CARDBOARD

THE TELLINGS OF ONE DAY IN NEW YORK CITY

COFFINS

A NOVEL BY SEANIE SUGRUE

Cardboard Coffins
by seanie sugrue

ISBN: 1729521258
ISBN-13: 978-1729521250

*Book design, type formatting, editing and illustration by
Amanda Martin.*

First published in the United Stated in 2018.

This book is dedicated to New York City,

for years of frequent demoralization and infinite inspiration.

Writers Note

Thank you to all the actors and crew I've had the pleasure of working with at Locked in the Attic Productions over the years. I've learned from all of you and cherish the time we've spent together creating art.

When I first started writing I had an audience of one, Amanda Martin. I would send her a play and she would always respond saying that it was great (even when it wasn't). Her support is what motivated me to become a writer that writes, not one that merely talks about writing. She is also my editor and drew all the art you'll see along the way.

Here is our book. It's a love story, it's a comedy and at times a tad tragic. For the easily offended, don't quit before the miracle happens.

1.

Sweet Phillip

The sun burned through the curtainless window from the glass all the way down to my face, blinding me as I tried to open an eye. My mouth felt like sandpaper and the little saliva that remained caused my face to stick to the stained and undressed mattress. I used what little energy I had left to pick up the dirty white sheet from the floor, pulling it up over my worthless piece of shit head. Masking myself was a temporary solution to my many permanent problems.

What time is it?
Do I have to work today?
What day is it?

These were all very familiar questions that didn't have any viable answers. It became evident, from the wet patch between my legs, that I'd pissed myself again.

My cracked iPhone screen was sticking out of the side pocket of my jeans on the floor seven feet away, but it may as well have been seven miles. The jeans were about as clean as the sheet, torn and covered with unexplained stains. I gave up while attempting to crawl towards them, it was more of a consideration than an actual attempt. Sitting to my left was another suicide note I'd written to my sister Mitten.

I'm sorry for everyone I caused you.

A fucking typo in my own suicide letter, accompanied by a half assed sad faced stick figure with a black and white hat on.

The window holding the air conditioner was also unattainable, like the jeans and cell phone. I knew there was a remote but like my mind and everyone around me, it was gone. Maybe the rat took it? Some nights I can hear it squeaking at the end of my mattress. Mitten once told me that a healthy rat is generally silent and they'll only squeak when they're ill. I vomited on the floor, intentionally over another pool of puke that was there from before.

I glanced at the picture of my dead mother hanging on the wall and thought about how lucky we both were that she wasn't around to see me. What would she say if she could look at me now? She'd nicknamed me Sweet Philip when I was a kid because I was effervescent. I wondered what happened to him, to me? The enthusiastic eleven-year-old striving to be the next Paul McCartney, banging on his guitar. She wasn't in any position to be judgmental, considering what she did to herself.

Sometimes I think about coloring her eyes in with black Sharpie so she can't look at me, so I don't have to look at her.

She taught me what it meant to be empty. Being desolate wasn't just an old cliché people threw around to sound deep, it meant not giving a fuck about anyone but yourself, to be incapable of loving anyone. Sometimes I'd stand on the edge of the Triboro where she jumped to clear my mind, a futile endeavor to feel closer to her.

I thought about trying to retrieve the iPhone from the side pocket of the dirty jeans seven miles away on the floor for a second time. This was interrupted by a sharp pain going through my neck, to my head, and to the interior of my two eyeballs causing me to audibly groan. I fell asleep again, this time having a nightmare about yellow Gatorade.

Walking through the desert, parched with thirst, I came across a half empty bottle of yellow Gatorade. Upon opening it, I was haunted to discover that it was full of Renee Zellweger's urine. I'm not sure why I assumed it was hers but I drank it.

They talked about incomprehensible demoralization at the AA meetings. As far as demoralization went, it felt as if I was starting to overachieve. I wanted something real, I wanted to be real, or something.

"Just one drink." I said talking to myself out loud trying to stay awake. "One to slow the fucking misery and that's it, never again."

On the third effort, I crashed head first to the floor landing in both pools of vomit. It was 11:58 am on

Wednesday, August 13th. I had twelve percent battery and one missed call from Mitten. My shift at the bar began at noon and it was impossible to get there on time. There was a crushed pack of cigarettes in the back pocket of the jeans with six smokes and my blue and orange Islanders lighter in it, three of them were broken in half and the rest were flattened, but still smokable. I lit one and tried to smoke it but the first drag made me light headed and nauseous. It was time to call Dave.

Dave was the owner of the bar I worked at. A month back he demoted me to only working days because I was allegedly getting too intoxicated on the job.

I was lying on the floor in Bed Stuy and needed to get from Brooklyn to the East Village. It was going to take at least another twenty minutes to get off the floor and another two or three to get ready for work. The train would be delayed since the MTA are a pack of cunts and I still needed to buy a beer to survive the commute. It was going to be one o'clock before I could get there. I closed my eyes and fell asleep.

12:45 pm. I was still lying naked, uninspired and persecuted on the bedroom floor. The short nap was tainted with anxiety and the smell of piss. It was now certainly time to call Dave.

He didn't pick up, but my brief moment of relief was spoiled as he called me right back. I ignored the call, but the anxiety from seeing his name on the screen got me off the floor. I stumbled down the hallway to the bathroom and took a piss in the sink. The toilet hadn't been functional in months and the last thing I needed was my landlord seeing how I lived my life.

While pissing, a rat started squeaking, no, screaming at me from the floor. He was in the corner stuck to a glue trap that I didn't remember setting, looking up at me with two bloodshot eyes.

"Who the fuck are you?" I said to him.

He squeaked louder this time really showing off his despair. Much quieter, he attempted to release himself. He struggled. Maybe it was a she? She fought good and hard but remained glued. That was the last fucking thing I needed, a rat fighting for its life on my bathroom floor.

Staring in the mirror, the only resemblance I could see between who I was and who I had become was my ex-girlfriend's name tattooed on my chest.

I wished I was the fucking rat. The reflection highlighted my yellow STD ridden face, an intravenous drug user without a will to live.

The black t-shirt lying on the floor was the cleanest one I had so I put it on. Dave tried calling again. I put my head under the faucet and glugged the lukewarm water for as long as I could hold my breath. The rat started squeaking even louder than before so I graciously closed the bathroom door on my way out.

As I re-entered my bedroom on the hunt for a semi-clean pair of socks, a second rat was standing on the mattress staring at me unfazed.

Who needs socks anyway?
Where did all these fucking rats come from?
What do they want from me?

"Fuck this, I'm leaving!" I said to him and like his kin in the bathroom he wasn't much of a conversationalist.

A rat stuck to a glue trap in the bathroom was one thing, but a rat running around the house like he owned the place was another. I made the decision that the infestation I was living in was no longer my apartment. By now I was so far behind on rent that it didn't matter if I lost the months deposit.

Using an empty box of cornflakes from the overflowing garbage can in the kitchen, I picked up the rat in the bathroom. After putting her in her cardboard coffin, I tossed it out the kitchen window. I put a pair of boxers and the picture of my mother in an old hockey gear bag, figuring my buddy Jimmie wouldn't mind me crashing on his couch for a while.

The walk to my new life was unsettling, plagued with intermittent headaches, signs that I was starting to get more sober with every step. Memories from the four-day cocaine-prostitute fueled bender began to resurface.

Did I really leave my ex-girlfriend that voicemail?
Did I pay any of those bar tabs?
I know there was some arguing but did I really hit that cab driver?

The anxiety was getting so severe that it started to send debilitating shivers down my spine. I transitioned from walking fast to running towards the nearest bodega. I grabbed the first can of whatever beer was closest and drank it right there in the aisle. I didn't have to look in my pockets to know that there wasn't a dime in them. I stuffed a second can down my pants and walked out the front door. The sound of an angry man yelling caused me to transition once more, this time sprinting towards the Gates subway station. After jumping the turnstile, another fool started screaming at me, this time from a glass box.

I walked along the yellow line to the end of the platform and sat on a wooden bench. The homeless man jerking off next to me didn't make me feel any better about my situation. Despite the train taking nearly twenty minutes, neither the fool in the box or a police officer approached me.

Posted on the wall behind us was a picture of six women and a guy that were missing. They had all disappeared over the course of the last two months. I wished I could vanish like them.

1:26 pm. I was eighty-six minutes late for work and could finally hear the train coming. I stuck my head out and imagined what it would feel like to kiss it, just once. I could feel the warm wind from the train in my face as it got closer. If I'd wanted to die, I would have done it already. I would have done it last night after writing that disgrace of a suicide letter. That's not to say I had any intention of living my life either.

Once, I was the lead singer of a decent band and we toured the country. I played all fifty states, twice, but shit happens, life is devastating and sometimes even Rock n Roll can get in the way of drinking. Unlike me, one of the other guitar players had what it took and killed himself in a charming motel in Ohio. That was the end of the band and my solo career hadn't exactly taken flight either. My most recent EP, *Jolene Just Jumped* dropped a year earlier and tanked. I clutched the name on my chest and wished I'd never met her.

After two stops on the train I noticed a beautiful girl sitting across from me. I eyed her up and she looked back. I smiled at her and she smirked. I offered her a sip of my beer and she said no.

"How about a drag of my cigarette then?" I asked and she declined.
"They could give you a ticket you know?"
"I don't pay those things anyway." I could tell she was impressed by my anarchy.

We kept chatting and it turned out she had been a drummer in a punk band when she was a teenager. Her name was Tammy and she was an aspiring actress. New in town, she was still finding her way around New York. After many failed auditions she was forced to take a shit job working at a health store in Queens.

As we continued to bond, the masturbating homeless cunt that had been jerking off beside me on the subway platform interrupted us. He was dressed in an *I Love the Bronx* t-shirt and had a patchy red beard.

"Look at me, I'm majestic." He said moving toward Tammy.

I told the dweeb to fuck off and he responded by poking me in the chest. Retaliation came quick as I punched him in the face, twice. Sometimes I'd surprise myself. I apologized to Tammy and walked off the train before anyone could report me. He deserved it. The guy was a creep that had been touching himself, claiming to be majestic.

I had no choice; trying to rationalize it.

2:53 pm. I arrived at *Patrick's Irish Pub*. That's what it's called, *Patrick's Irish Pub*, because apparently people wouldn't figure out it was Irish or a pub if it was simply called *Patrick's*. I'd been working there for a year and a half and I fucking hated it, the walls, the ceiling, the fucking assholes that drank there.

Then there was Dave, I struggled sometimes to put into words what I thought of him. The vocabulary to describe him didn't exist yet. Perhaps if I learned German or Dutch there'd be more appropriate words to portray him. Humans need air, food and water to survive. Dave is different. Dave's sole requirement was recognition. He needed to be told how great he was or else he would go out seeking it.

His father Patrick died a few years ago from HIV. He left Dave the bar and as a result now considered himself a roaring success. He reminded us about the hard times, when he didn't have a pot to piss in. He talked down to his staff like we were all peasants that he had pulled up from the gutter. Rumor had it, Dave lived with a case of erectile dysfunction so severe that not even Cialis could save him. He was standing at the door waiting for me with his chest puffed out and collar popped. Dave's all too familiar stance.

"You fucking stink and you're late, why are you always fucking stinking and late?!" he screamed.

We never had any customers before four, with the exception of Billy Bigley the alcoholic cop, but I kept my head down anyway and apologized.

"Sorry Dave, it'll never happen again man. I have deodorant downstairs." I said while dreaming of better

9

days when I could punch him like I did the man in the *I Love the Bronx* t-shirt.

"Wipe down all the bottles, the bars a fucking mess!" He screamed before going home to his unfulfilled wife.

While you may admire my restraint, the truth is unemployment meant not having any money to spend on hookers and blow.

I made my way behind the bar and poured myself a double house gin in a rocks glass, no ice. While downing it, I regretted not pouring myself something better. The next fifteen minutes were spent alternating between puking and lying on the bathroom floor. I poured myself another double, Bombay Sapphire this time and downed it in one. Finally, Sweet Philip was ready to work.

We still had no customers, not even the drunkard Billy Bigley. My shift ended at eight so the only chance I had of making any money was by robbing the place blind, and I fully intended on doing so. I needed two hundred dollars by eight o'clock, forty to tip Jimmie, who would let me drink for free all night, fifty for a bag of blow and at least a hundred for the strip club.

4:37 pm. I got my first and last customer of the day. He was six foot four and so big that juicing on steroids could be the only explanation. He was bald and wearing a ridiculous purple skinny scarf. He asked me for the whiskey menu but by the time I'd brought it to him he decided a water would suffice and asked to see the food menu instead. I threw it on the bar in front of him with absolutely no pride in my work. I poured myself another gin and downed it right in front of him. Gaining that bald fucker with a skinny scarfs' validation wasn't on my list of things to do. My eye was on the prize and the prize was cheap women, booze and cocaine. They can say what they want about me but my priorities were always straight.

The baldy fucker continued to run his mouth and my patience was wearing thin. He told me his name but I chose not to retain such a useless piece of information.

"I'm Phil, what the fuck do you want?" I responded abusively and he asked what kind of cheese we had. "The regular kind." I said even more rude than before. "I'll have an American burger, medium rare, deluxe." "Sure brother, whatever the fuck you want." I said shaking my head and grabbed the menu from his fat fingers.
"Make sure the cheese is low in fat." He yelled, twice.

I looked directly at him while taking an excessively large swig from the bottle. While wiping the gin from my chin I put the order in muttering something offensive and loud enough for him to hear it.

"Do you realize that the smell coming off of you is disgusting?"
"No one else seems to have taken issue with it." I said.

He took a look around the empty bar and back at me. The condescending prick. It was obvious he was jealous of my long flowing locks. I hadn't had a haircut in a year, but his comparisons were his problem.

I walked outside to get some fresh air and bummed a cigarette off some college girl in gym clothes. I thought about giving my sister Mitten a call, but my phone was still charging behind the bar. I'd call her tomorrow, I thought.

Once I got back behind the bar the bald fucker with the skinny scarf had his burger in front of him but hadn't taken a bite. I could feel myself getting depressed from the gin so I poured myself a bourbon to take the edge off. I'm not sure if it was Jack or Makers, but I definitely vomited in the trash can after drinking it. The baldy fuck was still staring at me while tapping the bar with his sausage fingers trying to get my attention.

"What the fuck is wrong with you?" I asked him wiping the vomit from my chin.
"Are you not going to bring me any condiments?"
"No."
"Cutlery?"
"Absolutely not." I responded and took a bite of his burger and dropped it on the bar in front of him.
"I'm not paying for this shit man, you're a fucking disaster." He said wrapping his skinny scarf around his bald head.
"Listen bro, either you're paying or we're fighting." I hoped he would pick the aforementioned.
"You do realize you're an alcoholic right?"

I'd heard this shit before.

"You need to find God and have a spiritual awakening." He preached.
"How about this for a fucking God?!" I screamed at him at the top of my lungs picking up his half empty glass of water and smashing it on the floor in front of him.

As the sound of broken glass rang around the bar, I noticed Dave walking in from the corner of my eye. He didn't say anything at first, but he did say something after I smashed the plate and the burger on the floor. Dave seemed petrified and the bald fucker looked absurd in his skinny scarf, but me, I was feeling a lot better.

"That's it, you're gone this time you fucking degenerate." Dave yelled at me while attempting to clean the bald fuckers' suit with a bar rag.
"Dave, you're being ridiculous." I said.
"Get the fuck out of my bar!" He screamed.

As he followed the baldy scarf wearing shithead to the bathroom I grabbed every dollar from the register and a bottle of gin. Four hundred dollars cash and Tanqueray, I was set. I grabbed my hockey bag and before leaving took a piss against the front door, a farewell gift for Dave. I put my dick back in my pants and walked out of *Patrick's Irish Pub* for the last time.

5:11 pm. I needed drugs. Coke or ecstasy, something. I needed a place to stay too. If I showed up at Jimmie's bar with my pockets full of blow, he'd let me crash at his place for sure. Jimmie didn't start his shift until seven so I had some time to find drugs first. My usual dealer cut me off because my tab was up to nearly a grand. I made my way over to Tompkins Square Park.

Buying coke in New York City was easy but getting the good stuff can be challenging, especially when you're looking for it at five o'clock in the afternoon. When I got to the park there were two black guys with their shirts off listening to rap music on an old school boombox.

Bingo.

"Cut the shit fellas, I've got forty bucks and I want a bag
of the good stuff."
"What the fuck are you talking about white boy?" The
larger one responded as I took a swig from my bottle of
gin.
"Is he always such an asshole?" I said to the less big of
the two drug dealers with the boombox.
"Do you think we're drug dealers because we're black?"
He asked.
"No." I responded. "I think you're drug dealers because
you don't have shirts on, you're in Tompkins Square
Park listening to Biggie Smalls on a fucking boombox
from the 1990's, and you're black."
The bigger of the two had me in a headlock on the
ground for what felt like an hour.
"Okay okay, you're not selling drugs, I get it!"

After he released me, I walked away. I'm no brain
surgeon but I am smart enough to know not to start a
fight with two black guys dealing drugs in Tompkins
Square Park. After thirty joyless minutes walking around
the park looking for a dealer, I was finally approached
by a midget wearing a pillowcase. She had heard me
talking to the two guys with the boombox and told me
that she had exactly what I was looking for.

"I have exactly what you're looking for." She said.

She was about three and a half feet high and her left foot
was noticeably wider than the other.

"What do you need?" She asked.
"Hard drugs, a lot of them and I want the good stuff,
none of that baking soda bullshit." I said with dominance
waving my finger at her lopsided forehead.

"I only sell the good stuff, that's why they call me Bunny Goodstuff."
"Give me a hundred dollars' worth of cocaine." I demanded and she laughed.
"You fucking hipster." She said walking away.
"Where are you going?!" I yelled hurrying after her.

All she had was heroin for ten dollars a bag. I didn't like needles and she told me to stop being a dirty pussy.

"Just sniff it then you dirty pussy."

I had never been spoken to like that by someone wearing a pillowcase.

"Alright fuck it, give me two bags then." I said and handed her a twenty.
"I'll give you four for thirty and a sip of that gin." She said pulling two more bags from her pillowcase.

I handed her the bottle.

On top of being a prolific drug dealer, Bunny told me that she was a very well-respected prostitute and promised me a good price for her services. Luckily, I wasn't that desperate.

6:00 pm. I had an hour to go before Jimmie started work. I found a park bench near Avenue B and got out the first of the four bags of dope. It looked a lot like coke except it was brown and cheap as shit. I pulled a People Magazine out of the trash can, grabbed a twenty-dollar bill and started sniffing dope right there on the corner of Avenue B.

The sun started to set, it was evening.

I woke up shaking and covering in my own vomit after being on one of the greatest highs of my life. I regretted all the money I'd wasted on cocaine. Heroin was the future. I could see from a clock on a high building that Jimmie was finally at work.

On my way out of the park, I ran into Bunny again. She was attractive in a peculiar sort of way. She had seductive eyes. She asked me where I was going and when I told her about Jimmie's free bar, she invited herself along. Fuck it, I thought to myself, drinking with a midget drug dealer was better than being alone.

This was the first mistake of my day.

When we got to the bar Jimmie didn't appear overjoyed to see us. He wanted to have a word with me in the kitchen and it seemed serious.

"Who the fuck is yer wan?" He threw at me.

He meant Bunny. Jimmie was from Dublin and I could hardly understand a word he said.

"It's Bunny Goodstuff bro, everyone knows that." I said hoping he wouldn't ask about the pillowcase.
"You look like fucking shite." He said grabbing my piss stained shirt as an example.
"Physically I'm feeling pretty good."
"You were in here last night acting the bollix, loaded on your tobler. You took a slash against the bar and didn't leave a fucking bob down." [Translation: You were here last night, drunk, by yourself and urinated against the bar counter. You didn't leave any money.]
"Why are you being so judgmental?" I asked and handed him a couple of twenties.

"I wonder where you got this?" Talking down to me.
"What's that supposed to mean?"
"I spoke to Dave you fucking clown. He told me you showed up to work four hours late, got into a scrap with some baldy fucker at the bar and robbed four hundred dollars from the till."
"I was only three hours late."

I paused.

"Listen man, you think I could crash on your couch for a while?"
"Are you fucking kidding me?"
"Two- or three-days tops."
"I have a ball and chain and a toddler at the gaff, look at the state of you for fuck's sake." [Translation: I have a wife and a child at home, you are in no condition to be around them.]
"I have nowhere else to go."
"Go stay with dat auld dirty ten-dollar hooker you're riding."
[Translation: Crash at Brandy's.]

Brandy Bones was a forty-six-year-old stripper I'd met in Long Island City a week earlier. Despite telling me that she loved me, it didn't seem realistic that she would let me move in with her. Before I could argue my case, we heard the sound of glass and barstools crashing.

Bunny was standing over some girl she had destroyed with a wine glass. Before Jimmie or myself could break it up, she beat her over the head five or six times with an ashtray. Despite the smoking ban, Jimmie liked to put ashtrays on the bar for authenticity purposes, a decorative decision he undoubtedly now regretted. The girl's skull had caved in on the right-hand side and her jaw looked broken. Turns out she was Jimmie's new girlfriend.

"That's my new fucking bird!" He yelled.
"I thought you were married?"
"What the fuck Phil?!" He screamed.
"I didn't do anything."
"You brought that fucking psychopath in here!" He howled.

While we were arguing, Bunny was on the floor cutting off the young woman's top lip with what was left of the broken wine glass. I vomited on the floor.

"Jesus fucking Christ!"

Jimmie grabbed Bunny by the hair and dragged her across the floor towards the door. I spread the vomit around with my foot and grabbed the bag with the picture of my dead mom. At that point Bunny had broken free and pointed what was left of the wine glass at Jimmie.

"Get your hands off my pussy you fucking cunt!" Bunny screamed.

Jimmie and I looked at one another and forced Bunny into my hockey bag. I was furious and didn't let her out until we got to Avenue A. The little bitch cost me a seat at my favorite drinking establishment and a couch to sleep on. I gave her the silent treatment and snorted another line of heroin. She sat in the grass. We both stayed quiet for a half an hour without saying a word.

8:15 pm. I finally broke the silence. "He shouldn't have been cheating on his wife like that."

I forgave Bunny, I mean who was I to pontificate pacifism after the week I had. The worst part was that I'd given Jimmie the forty bucks right before he flipped out on me. Bunny told me that the girl had a cavalier attitude and was staring at her very condescendingly, so the homewrecker wasn't totally innocent either.

The sun was set but it was still close to one hundred degrees in the park. Bunny took off her pillowcase and laid naked with me in the grass. We stared at the one star shining in the sky and Bunny named it Savage. The moonlight lit up Bunny's naked body and I couldn't help but feel aroused. I took her hand and placed it on my dick and she began jerking me off. One thing leads to another and we were having sex.

Afterwards she told me I could have fucked her for free, but since I came inside her she wanted twenty-seven dollars for medication. After the transaction we parted ways. I walked back to my bench, snorted some more of Bunny's dope and passed out.

9:20 pm. I woke up to the sound of multiple rats squeaking beneath me. I could still see Savage in the sky and couldn't help but feel sentimental that Bunny was gone.

I thought it was weird that Brandy Bones hadn't called me all day. I sent her a text.

Hey Brandy! I'm horny and I have heroin. Do you like heroin? Have you done heroin? Can't go back to my place, there's rats and the toilet still isn't working. Can we go to yours? I got fired today so I don't have any money to go to the club, so how about I just come over? Call me.

I did another line of heroin and Brandy text me back.

Phil! I'm working all night. I'll call you tomorrow, love you!

I was officially homeless. I walked back to St. Marks Place and booked a hotel for the night. The staff all knew me. They had hourly rates but tonight I was there for the long haul. Fred at the desk booked me into my usual room and told me I didn't have to pay him until the morning.

The rooms were tiny, there was a streak of blood in the shape of a heart on the wall and the curtains were stained with semen. I sat on the floor and thought about the last few months. If only I'd treated Samantha a little better and hadn't cheated on her with all of those hookers. I thought about removing her name from my chest.

I walked into the bathroom and smashed the mirror. The crash of the glass sounded so good that I punched it again cutting my hand open. I wrapped it with a towel and snorted another line but the pain didn't go away. I began trashing the hotel room to distract myself from the bleeding. I kicked the TV screen in, tore all of the art off the walls and went at the bathroom mirror again. Seven years of bad luck, just what I needed. I took the picture of my mother out from my bag and hung it up on the bathroom wall where the mirror once was. I sat in the middle of the broken glass and looked up at her.

What now Mom?
What did you expect?
What's Fred at the desk going to say about this?

I was in a bar in Astoria when Mitten called me with the news.

"Mom's dead." That's all she said.
"How's she dead?" I asked.
"She fell."
"She fell or she jumped?"
"It doesn't matter." She said and hung up.

The sound of my phone ringing shook me out of my trance. It was Samantha. I'm not sure why but I answered it.

"Phil?"
I couldn't think of anything to say.
"You need help." Samantha's two cents before hanging up to only the sound my breath.

There was an AA meeting around the corner from the hotel. My mom went there back in the day before she lost her mind. I knew there was a meeting around ten. I'd be late but figured what the hell and walked over there regardless.

This was my second mistake.

10:45 pm. I did my last line before leaving the hotel. By the time I got to the meeting I could hardly keep my eyes open. It felt like everyone was staring at me so I sat in the back. I nodded off as soon as I sat in the chair. It seemed like a dream.

The next thing I remember was waking up on the sidewalk, bleeding with a swollen face. While I was trying to find my bearings, I noticed the silhouette of a man standing over me. He was wearing a shirt that read *I Love the Bronx.* The homeless man from the J train had got payback for my short-tempered madness. As he walked away, I noticed the bald fucker with a skinny scarf yelling something at someone and shit started to get confusing. Men dressed in police uniforms ran by me only adding to my confusion. The gun shots didn't phase me. I walked back to the hotel.

Back at the room I emptied my pockets and came to the sad realization that it was over. The drugs were gone, the money was gone, the job was gone and all hope was lost. I took off my shirt and picked up a piece of glass from the floor and tried to cut the S in Samantha off my chest. The ink didn't come off but the blood was covering it at least. My phone started vibrating again. I had a text from Mitten.

I love you.

I didn't respond, instead I decided to take advantage of the rooms embellishments and run myself a bath.

I picked up another piece of glass from the floor and got in the tub still wearing my dirty blue jeans. Finally, they were clean. I could see my cracked iPhone on the ground about seven feet away.

11:58 pm. Wednesday, August 13th. With twelve percent battery I cut my left wrist, down the road not across the street, someone said once. The incision ran from where I once wore a wrist watch all the way up to my elbow. I switched hands and did the same to the right. The water in the bathtub went from looking like a vodka soda with a splash of cranberry to a full-bodied cherry wine. I thought about Samantha and all her fucking ultimatums. I didn't have to worry about her now.

I told her once that she'd miss me when I was gone.

I wondered if she would miss me when I was gone.

I could see my mother standing over me smiling, everything was going to be okay now. Mitten was going to be better off without me, Mom and I knew it and eventually Mitten would come to know it too.

What was the point of all this bullshit?
Am I going somewhere after this?
Do humans really have this much blood?

I start to feel tired, so fucking tired that I can't keep my eyes open any longer, so I close them. This feels good. I feel good. For the first time today, for the first time in weeks and the first time in years, I feel good. I hear the water pouring from the faucet and the sound of it flowing over on to the floor.

It stops.

I can't hear anything at all.

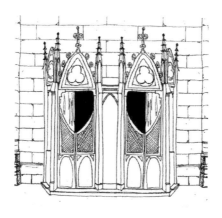

2.

House of Gains

The alarm went off. I hit the button as fast as I could so it wouldn't wake up my sloppy wife lying next to me, looking like a beached whale. I wished she was dead. The repugnant animal. She groaned but didn't wake up. The only reason we were in the same bed was out of spite.

"Why should I sleep on the fucking couch?!" I'd yelled at her the night before expressing my discontent. I added, "You may have bought all the furniture but I paid for the sheets, so take your ass to the couch, or better yet the bathtub!"

It had been a rough night with unavoidable consequences which included a hickey a young babe left on my neck, but that didn't need to be dealt with again, at eight o'clock in the morning.

Dorothy let out a loud boarish snore while I tried to escape captivity. I did my best to keep the noise down. I was able to get out of the bedroom by restricting my movements. Standing on the other side of the door I caught my breath and thought about Candi's long steamy legs. She exuded a divine exquisiteness when she wore those short skirts, silky and soft. Her fishnet tights with intentional holes were so enticing.

I've hated both of my kids since the day they were born and would have traded them for a box of cereal. My son, who I have disowned, is gay and doesn't even have a gym membership. My daughter is a walking drama queen, like her mother. She goes to school in Virginia and hasn't come home in over a year. As for my wife Dorothy, she was lucky she was still breathing after her antics the night before. Now all that might seem a bit despicable, but it's the truth.

Normally I would wake up, pump iron and go to my health store *House of Gains* to do the books, but not today. Last year I caught a kid trying to steal pre-workout and ended up breaking his jaw, so today I had to go to the courthouse. I'm close to three hundred pounds and could be described as an animal at times.

The kid was about a buck fifty, seventeen years old and didn't stand a chance against a man of my magnitude. I had to protect my business and sometimes you have to make an example out of people. First, it's a kid stealing pre-workout, before you know it, you've got the whole of Queens robbing you blind.

This was my first day away from the store in weeks. My manager Susie Jones, who's in love with me, stopped showing up a couple of weeks ago and I started questioning her loyalty toward me. We had a falling out after I enforced a rule that made it mandatory for all staff to wear tight sports bras and short shorts while working. She found this disrespectful to women. It was no coincidence that the one chick at the store who had a less than ideal figure took issue with the new guidelines. She should have spent more time on the treadmill and less reading feminist weekly. The real issue of course was that I'd got sick of having sex with her and this was her way of revolting against me. When you have a lot of money and a full head of hair on your head you can have any girl you want. Of course, when you're in my position you're not going to settle with one little whore like Susie Jones.

"What's the point of cheating on your wife if you're going to do it with the same chick over and over?" I'd asked her before she vanished without a trace.

The cops stopped by the store a week earlier saying that Susie's family had filed a missing person report, but I knew it was all an act to make me feel something toward her.

Every successful man knows that you should never just settle for one mistress. John F Kennedy didn't cheat on Jackie solely with Marilyn Monroe, he had an entire smoke show entourage. You have to rotate them like a baseball coach rotates his pitchers. Winning teams have strong starters and an even stronger bullpen. I didn't move all the way from Delaware to New York City to put up with some eighteen-year-old bitch complaining.

I found a part time manager Crystal who was only sixteen years old and looked great in her bra and short shorts. I'd already promised to buy her a bottle of whiskey and take her out for her seventeenth birthday next month, but only if she wears the *House of Gains* uniform. She was promiscuous and looked electrifying in those short shorts, so sensational in fact that her promotion was justifiable, though I was disappointed when I read on Facebook that she had been hanging out with an aspiring actor.

I headed to the bathroom to apply *U.A.F* to my scalp. *Unstoppable Astronomical Follicle* had changed my life since I'd started using it a few months earlier. I'd regained most of my hair and the will to live. Almost forty years I spent bald and now thanks to this miracle potion I'd grown a full influential head of hair. Cheating on my wife went from an occasional pastime to a regular way of life. I could tell people were inspired by me. The *U.A.F* cost two thousand dollars for an eight-ounce bottle and even though I would use it sparingly, my wife still criticized me for it. The deceitful walrus.

"You're throwing my money down the drain!" She'd yell and even had the nerve to tell me that it wasn't working, despite the locks being so rich and notable.

After applying the potion, I couldn't risk waking up the gruesome dragon by getting dressed so I went to the spare room to find an outfit. The suit I married Dorothy in was hanging in the closet and I figured, why not? I put on one of her scarves to cover the hickey on my neck.

My AA sponsor had also assisted me over the years with my new-found comfort. We worked the twelve steps together and he helped me develop a close connection with my higher power. I had a spiritual awakening and I highly recommend it.

After the extraordinary mane regrowth and the incident with the thief at my store, my sponsor became jealous and judgmental. He misdirected his emotions and dropped me as his sponsee, citing that I wasn't being rigorous about my program or with my connection.

"If you're not going to start taking your sobriety serious, I'm not working with you anymore." He would threaten.

He left and I'd wished he had taken my wife and kids with him.

Eight years sober, getting into fist fights on the street, cheating on my horrible dog of a wife with teenage girls and prostitutes wasn't sober behavior in his small-minded opinion. The man was married for twenty years and claimed he never once cheated. I wondered how he had hidden his blatant homosexuality from her for so long. Shortly after he dropped me, I met my sweet chick Candi who changed my life forever, with those legs.

Candi was the hottest girl on this side of the Mississippi River. She worked as a hooker five nights a week and she was mine the other two, all seven if I was willing to pay the piper and she was worth it when I did. Her idol was Mary Magdalene and claimed that prostitution was the world's oldest profession. A few months ago, she seduced me after an AA meeting and we hit it off. She had been sober for close to eight years and worked a strong program. Candi was an intelligent, strong minded woman that spoke passionately about World War Two. Occasionally, we'd even go to mass at St. Patrick's Cathedral together. There's a saying, sweating like a whore in church, but that didn't ring true for Candi. She walked out of there bone dry every Sunday.

There was one exception.

A few weeks after we met, we were at mass and passion got the better of us. After the crowd dispersed, I handed Candi a wad of cash telling her that I needed her right then and there. She took the money and I put my hand up her dress. She always wore a long black dress on Sundays.

"Follow me." She said, and I did.

She started going down on me. At first, we had no idea someone else was in the confession box with us, until we heard it.

"Hello, child of God." A goddamn priest in the box while my rock-hard cock was in Candi's mouth only a few feet away.

Candi took my dick out of her mouth and I forced it back in, like a virgin in a dress could keep those succulent lips off my pecker.

"Bless me Father for I have sinned, it has been thirty-two years and eight months since my last confession." I conceded trying to hold back the laughter. "I have been mean to my wife sir, you know?"
"I see." The priest said and I could tell that I was moments away from finishing.
"I've been unfaithful to her Father."
"There's another woman?"
"There is Father, a prostitute."

Candi tried to pull away again but I kept those lips where they needed to be. The moment finally got to me and I blew my load all over Candi. She was pissed. I had paid her nine hundred dollars, what did she expect? Twenty-two Hail Mary's later and a fiver in the collection basket, I was absolved.

Candi insisted that I pay her more money for forcing myself on her and that she didn't want to see me again until I did. It was during this brief intermission that I started riding Susie on the side. A poor man's Candi. After a week or two I showed up at Candi's apartment with ten grand in cash and she took me back. That was the same week Susie took off. Candi may have been a woman of the night, but once I left Dorothy, she was going to come work with Crystal and I at *House of Gains*. She would quit the stripping and whoring business altogether and she would be mine, exclusively.

Eating breakfast wasn't an option, I had to get out of the house before Dorothy woke up and attacked me again. Before I left, I stepped on a piece of glass that was still on the floor from when she threw the wine bottle. This kind of violence was nothing out of the ordinary. Dorothy was often turbulent when she drank.

I'd been hanging out with a young babe that would have looked great in a *House of Gains* uniform the night before. I'd met her at the store a few weeks earlier looking for a hangover cure and talked her into coming to an AA meeting. I'd promised to take her out for a coffee and a good time afterward.

We discussed God, sobriety and what it all meant to me. I asked her about her favorite sex positions. I think her name was Mendy or Mitten, something like that. She had huge fake tits that were brand new and radiant. After the meeting, we were making out in the rain outside an Italian coffee shop when she left the infamous hickey on my neck. I wanted to slap her after realizing what she had done. That's not to say I didn't enjoy it, but I knew the blemish would cause a lot of domestic drama once I got back to the house. Her name was definitely Mitten, not Mendy, it felt inevitable that Mitten would be sucking on my cock like the ravenous reptile she was. As you probably guessed, my insecure wife started throwing accusations and wine bottles around as soon as I entered the house. I told her that it was my eczema acting up again but she didn't buy it.

She was a cheap bitch when it came to buying things like that.

I accidentally pushed her at one point banging her head off the door and then she really lost it.

"You put your hands on me you bastard." She growled. "Shut your fucking mouth!" I screamed back at her.

She was looking for any excuse to leave me, trying to make it like our failed marriage was my fault so I wouldn't be entitled to my fair half. When I noticed blood coming out of her left ear I felt concerned, but in my defense, she had said some very hurtful things. She always knew the most devastating ways to hurt me.

"You baldy piece of shit!" She'd scream despite the fact that I now had a full head of hair growing on my head.

I got out of the house undetected and drove to Manhattan.

Six months' probation and thirty thousand dollars compensation to cover hospital bills, the price for defending my store.

"It could have been worse." My overpaid lawyer told me. "At least you still have your business." Which was his way of saying he was worth the ten grand I paid him.

As much as I didn't want to admit it, he was right. *House of Gains* was still in operation and I wasn't going to prison. I could divorce Dorothy and spend the rest of my life living free from sin, fucking babes like Candi and once she turned seventeen, Crystal too. I'd already bought the birthday card and set a reminder in my iPhone. We would all work out together, eat grilled chicken with a little portion of quinoa and live a happy life full of honest penetration and seduction. If I dated both of them, the need to cheat would be far less, win win.

It was almost two before I got out of the courthouse and over 100 degrees in the city. I regretted not bringing a change of clothes but the scarf really complemented the outfit and my hair looked phenomenal slicked back. As I turned the corner on Chambers and Broadway, in route to my favorite massage parlor, my phone started beeping, a voicemail from Dorothy. I fell to my knees listening to her elephantine voice rumble.

"I know everything. I know all about that filthy hooker you've been running around with. I know how you got that hickey on your neck from that slut with the fake tits last night. I hired a private detective and she has videos and pictures of everything you've been doing for the last month. I'm filing for divorce and taking everything, the house, the kids, your stupid fucking sexist health store, the dogs, the turtle, everything you piece of shit." She started laughing ending it with, "You're going to be back in the gutter where you belong you stupid baldy bastard."

She always knew the most devastating ways to hurt me.

My initial reaction was why she thought I cared about the turtle or the fucking kids. The turtle spent most of its time in the dark and my kids were the worst things that ever happened to me. I was relieved that she hadn't mentioned anything about the pictures of Crystal in the changing room. I'd installed hidden cameras so the staff couldn't steal from me. There was one installed in the bathroom and another one in the back room where the girls changed. I'd spend hours watching the footage on my phone at night while my hippopotamus of a wife hibernated beside me. I was about to lose everything and there was no way Candi would stay with me if I didn't have anything. How could she? Crystal maybe, Susie definitely, but with Candi, not a chance.

"That fucking whore, cuntbag bitch!" I screamed to the sky at the top of my lungs.

Dorothy was always insecure, but conducting an investigation like this was ludicrous. How dare she invade my privacy and hire a detective to follow me. I wondered if it was someone I knew, could it have been one of my employees at the store that deceived me? Was it Susie Jones that threw me under the bus? The snakey rat.

Without Dorothy's financial support I wouldn't be able to afford my monthly subscription to *U.A.F.* I picked myself back up and continued walking in no particular direction. Dorothy had spiritually and emotionally bankrupt me, and soon the whore would financially destroy me too. I wouldn't see a dollar of her family's money if she had proof of my infidelity in the courtroom. The store had been losing money for years and without her financial backing its closure was imminent. Would this be the last time I'd ever get to touch a girl of Candi's stature in the flesh? I knew Dorothy was heartless but even for her, this was ruthless. She knew how much the growth meant to me.

I ended up in the East Village with an irreversible urge to get shitfaced. My AA home group was only a few blocks away, but I couldn't bring myself to go in. There were never any chicks at the day meetings and an AA meeting without chicks was like giving a goldfish a bicycle, pointless. Then it appeared before me like a fucking mirage, *Patrick's Irish Pub*. Despite being mainly Puerto Rican I like to tell people I'm half Irish.

I ran across the street through oncoming traffic, past the wooden doors and grabbed the first barstool. There weren't any customers other than myself. I liked to drink alone, especially when my wife was being a deceptive cow. After settling down I noticed that the bartender was alternating between puking in the trash can and drinking Bombay Sapphire out of the bottle. My kind of place. As I was about to order a pint of the black stuff and a triple shot of Powers Irish Whiskey, I received two text messages.

There was one from Candi.

See you tonight xxx.

She meant sexually. Candi's sexting had given me a much-needed moment of clarity. The other was from Crystal.

The cops were here. Also, we are out of toilet paper.

I looked at a naked picture I'd taken of Candi while she was sleeping. Her belly button was so provocative. I ordered a glass of water, to the bartenders' disappointment and asked to see a food menu. For some unexplained reason, I decided to continue to sit there.

The bartender's name was Phil and he looked like he had been living in pretty trying circumstances, maybe even worse than myself. I reflected on what my sponsor used to say.

What do you do when you're having the worst day of your life? Be of service and help other sick and suffering alcoholics.

Phil was certainly that. His shirt was covered in vomit stains and he smelled like a urinal. He finished the bottle of gin and poured himself a glass of whiskey.

There are no victims in Alcoholics Anonymous, only volunteers.

I wanted to stand up and leave but out of respect to my sponsor I stayed to try and be of service. The menu was limited, no healthy options, just fried and fatty everything. I decided to throw myself a cheat day and ordered a burger with low fat cheese. Phil, the inebriated bartender criticized my decision calling me a demanding cunt.

Some are sicker than others.

After he put my order in, Phil left the bar unattended and it felt as if he was never coming back. I took advantage of the solitude by taking a sip of my water and pulling out my dick at the bar. Once hard, I took a picture, cropping it so it was artistic and in black and white. I sent it to Candi and asked her if she missed it. I took another sip of my water and sent it to Susie Jones asking how much she craved it. Neither responded, maybe Susie really was missing. At first, I decided against sending it to Crystal since she wasn't turning seventeen for another month, but I sent it over to her too. I followed up with an apology text saying it wasn't for her but I knew she would be overjoyed by the artistic photo. I took another sip of my water. After fifteen minutes Phil still hadn't returned and I was beginning to get frustrated.

You have to want it to get it.

A foreigner brought me my burger and it looked disgusting. The fries were soaked in grease and the cheese didn't look like it was low in anything. Phil finally returned, pouring himself another glass of gin, Tanqueray this time, washing it down with a shot of Jack Daniels. The smell coming off of him was unbearable. I asked for utensils and he told me to go fuck myself. He picked up my burger and took a bite and spat his food out on the bar in front of me.

"That's it, I'm fucking leaving and I'm not paying for this shit." I told him and got up from my seat.

He got confrontational telling me that he was going to beat me up if I didn't pay him. This made me laugh, the guy looked like he hadn't been to a gym once in his life and I was on day 26 of my latest steroid cycle. I calmed myself down and told him to chill or it would end badly for him.

"You do realize you're a drug addict and an alcoholic right?" I asked him trying to be as compassionate as I could.
"Fuck off."

I told him he needed to get on his knees and pray to God for help and then he really lost it.

"How about this for a fucking God, you fucking cunt!" He screamed at me before throwing my glass of water on the floor and following it up with my plate, it was an incredible display of active alcoholism and rage.

Unfortunately for Phil, the owner arrived in the middle of his episode.

"That's it, you're fucking gone this time!" His boss yelled, indicating that this was not an unusual occurrence.

I went to the bathroom to dry off and the owner followed me downstairs.

"I'm sorry about him." He said as he dried my shirt with a rag. "He's a fucking idiot."
"He's a drug addict, have some compassion." I responded and could tell he was impressed. I don't believe he had ever seen someone carry out God's work in a real-life situation before. When we walked back upstairs, Phil was gone.

The owner's name was Dave. He was a skinny fat meat head who walked around with his chest stuck out like a pigeon. He looked like he may have lifted weights, twenty years ago. What annoyed me the most about him was that he acted like he identified with my huge arms and traps.

"What are you putting up?" He asked.

I was benching about three fifty but I told him five hundred because I knew I'd never run into him at a gym.

"I used to be putting up three or four hundred, but I put my shoulder out." He said.
"Sure you were."

He was a nice guy, despite his unbearable narcissism and low tolerance for his alcoholic drug addict bartender. He told me that when he was younger, he didn't have a pot to piss in but really got his life together since becoming financially successful, which I respected. On my way out, I couldn't help but notice the smell of piss and found the puddle Phil had left by the front door.

"That's it, he's fucking done now!" Dave yelled. "I'll call every fucking bar owner in the city."

Finally, Candi responded to my dick picture.

Don't forget to bring cash!

That was it? She didn't even mention the fucking photograph. I checked the store cameras on my phone and saw Crystal playing with her cell phone. Why hadn't she responded to my dick picture? There was nothing back from Susie either. The stupid bitch.

Candi was fucking some rich old guy and couldn't meet until six so I had some time to kill. I walked to Tompkins Square Park to clear my head, but two shirtless drug dealers were blasting rap music from a boombox so I had to move. God had tested me at the bar and He was doing the same in the park.

God will never throw anything at you that he doesn't think you're able to handle.

At six fifteen on the dot Candi walked up to me looking stunning and elegant. She was wearing high heels that really complimented her calf muscles and a short red dress showing off the rose tattoo covering most of her left thigh. Whenever I was feeling down, Candi would show up in a colorful dress and make me feel better. She could tell I was upset.

I filled her in on Dorothy's discovery and played the voicemail. While she was listening, I put my hand up her short dress and played with the fabric of her underwear. It was delightful. After listening to the voicemail, she told me we had nothing to worry about. She always knew what to say.

"Your wife is an idiot." She said erotically.

We discussed possible solutions and agreed that my hagfish of a wife was causing us serious problems. Candi conceptualized the plan.

"There's honestly only one option and you know what it is." She said, but I was so blinded by her cleavage that she had to repeat herself.

"There's honestly only one option and you know what it is." She said again.

I figured she meant go to the hotel, order Chinese food, have some sex and deal with all this later, but Candi was a radical thinker.

"Let's go back to your house in Queens, hold her down and slice her wrists open." She said spitting lust in my face as she talked.
"We can't kill her Candi."
She told me to keep my voice down.
"Why not?"
"Because I don't want to go to jail."

She explained that we would make it look like a suicide, forge the suicide letter and everything. I waited for her to laugh but she was dead serious. Her tits looked sensational in that red dress.

"You're still married. If she files for divorce with all that evidence you're fucked. That beautiful hair on your head will be gone, your store, gone."
"And you?" I asked.
"How could I stay?"
She couldn't.
"If she dies before any of this shit comes out, then we'll get everything."
"Kill her?" I struggled, still in disbelief.

She nodded her head, which caused her tits to bounce up twice. There were many doubters that questioned their legitimacy because of how large and sublimely unique they were, but Candi's breasts were one hundred percent the real fucking deal. I did hate Dorothy for forcing me into having kids, ultimately ruining my life, but killing someone was a little out of my range. I had morals, and the number one rule on my list of ethics was not murdering people.

Women are capable of doing unimaginable things to a man. They'll make you mow the lawn and throw your own mother down a flight of stairs at the same time. They give us a taste of it you see and once you've had that taste, you're toast.

"Why didn't you respond to my dick picture?" I asked her.

"I did."

"Asking me for money isn't a response. Did you enjoy it?"

"I loved it" She said wiping a tear from my eye. "I'll let you fuck me for the rest of the year for free, how about that? How does that sound?" She said opening her legs and touching my now hard as chrome cock.

We agreed that the best way to write the suicide note was through her Facebook account. I knew it would already be logged in on her phone, the literature was going to be the hard part. As for the murdering, I was going to hold her down while Candi took a blade to her arteries.

Candi's perfume smelled like cut grass in the fall and strawberry marshmallows over a campfire on Christmas Eve. I couldn't control how much I desired her. Now that Candi was mine exclusively, without any restrictions, I booked a room at an hourly rate hotel on St. Marks Place and we had sex for fifty-two minutes. While hammering her from behind, she would often cut her arm with a small knife.

"We'll need a much bigger weapon for we're doing." I told her and we both laughed.

After I came inside her, I cleaned my dick off on the curtains and told her I'd never get sick of banging her. I wouldn't allow her to shower, I always wanted her to smell like me, I always wanted to be inside her. She had cut her arm deeper than usual and we used her blood to draw a love heart on the wall.

"Okay, pay up." She said extending her hand.
"What? You're mine exclusively now."
"Not until that bitch is dead." She said.

I paid her in full. While Candi was in the bathroom, I checked my phone. Crystal finally text me back.

Hey, Tammy was supposed to be here two hours ago and there's no sign of her. What should I do? I have to leave now to get to class. Should I just close the store early? Please call me. No worries about the picture.

No worries? No fucking worries? That's it? I was livid. She barely acknowledged the fact that I'd sent her an artistic picture of my dick in black and white while it was as hard as a coffin nail. This sort of disrespect was exactly why I needed to stop hanging out with sixteen-year olds. As for Tammy, I wasn't surprised, she was a flaky actress from Arizona. I would have already fired her if not for the fact that I hadn't had sex with her yet. She looked great in our uniform, her tits weren't cannons but they had a fancy shape.

Cancel your class and stay at the store.

I checked the cameras to see what she was doing and was horrified to see her standing behind my counter with a zip up hoodie on covering my uniform. How the fuck

seanie sugrue

did she expect anyone to buy protein powder if they couldn't see her tits?

Take off that jacket and turn the fucking air conditioner off.

No worries about the dick pic.

After Candi and I left the hotel there was pandemonium outside of the bar next door. A girl with her top lip dangling off was being put in the back an ambulance. Her eurotrash boyfriend was screaming something about a midget in a pillowcase.

We got into Dorothy's car and drove to Queens. As we went over the 59th Street Bridge I grabbed Candi by the hair and she paid her dues. She charged me another four hundred dollars.

Once we got to the house we waited outside for an hour until we saw the lights go down. We figured it would be easier to kill her while she was asleep. I was nervous, but Candi was her usual calm, assuring me that she would take care of everything. It was nine pm by the time her bedroom lights went down and we were half naked making out.

"Okay, are you ready?" Candi asked me lustfully as she put her black bra back on.
"I'm ready baby." I responded staring at her tits under the streetlights.

Dorothy had changed the locks already so I had to climb through the window to get into my own fucking house. Once inside, I opened the door to let the dogs out and let Candi in. I held the door for her like a gentleman.

The first problem we encountered were the dogs, they wouldn't shut up. Candi picked a great knife that I had stolen from the Striphouse restaurant. It was about eleven inches long, serrated, and perfect for slaughtering my sea loin of a wife. The dogs were still barking outside and I could tell Candi wasn't happy about it. She walked by me and I couldn't help but be turned on by the sweat patch on her sexy lower back. She was still holding the knife on her way outside. The barking stopped. Candi walked back inside, her legs covered in blood.

"Remember to put something about the mutts in the suicide letter." She said and I could feel my penis erecting. We walked upstairs to the bedroom. The bedroom where we would murder my wife. The nasty rodent.

The floorboards were creaky so I told Candi to take off her six-inch-high heels. She had beautiful toes and her nail polish was red to match her short tight dress. I got on the ground and sucked on three of her toes.

"Later, we have to kill her first." Candi whispered as we peeked our heads through the door.

I could tell that Candi was judging me for marrying such a disgusting sloth.

"Wait here." Candi said on her tippy toes as she walked across the room. She grabbed Dorothy's phone from the nightstand and tiptoed back to me.

Before we did the deed, I updated Dorothy's Facebook status.

Hey guys, I love all of you and I think you all love me too. However, this crazy world has got too whacky for me and I can't go on. My beautiful husband, this isn't your fault, you're the only reason I've lasted as long as I have. You're the only one I've ever loved, I love you. D.

Candy made some grammar and punctuation corrections and we posted it. Right away it received a like which despite confusing me a little meant time was no longer on our side.

"You forgot the dogs." Candi whispered.

I posted a second status.

And I'm taking the dogs with me.

I ran across the room at full speed and leaped on top of Dorothy's back putting both of my knees on her shoulders to pin her down. Dorothy woke up and started screaming. I had to use both hands to cover her wide trout mouth.

The fear of death doesn't prevent them from dying, it merely prevents them from living. The only cure for fear is action.

"Now Candi, cut her!" I yelled.
"Oh, so you're orchestrating this now? Don't tell me what to do." Candi demanded cocking one hip and putting a fist on her waist, sexually.

Dorothy started biting my fingers so I elbowed her in the side of the head, nothing serious.

"Don't mark her!" Candi yelled.

"Just do it!"
"Shit, I forgot the knife!"

She had forgot to pick the knife back up after gutting the dogs.

"What the fuck do you mean you forgot it?" I said and the bitch bit me again.
"I'll be right back!" Candi yelled while running down the stairs.

That was the first and last time I've ever yelled at Candi.

By now I could feel Dorothy's tears on my hand and her heavy breathing was making them turn moist. I took my hands off her mouth as quick as I could to try and dry them. She muttered something indecipherable, which wasn't unlike her. I covered her mouth once more pressing harder this time. Candi ran back into the room holding the knife turning me on. I was hard as a brick wall.

"I'm sorry I yelled at you." I said.

We kissed passionately and I forced my wife to watch by grabbing her by the back of the head. This was the kind of payback I was looking for.

"Wait, let's enjoy this." Candi said. "Any last words for us Dorothy?"
"Grizzly bears can't talk Candi." I said and laughed.
"Let her speak."

I warned her that if she tried anything, I'd kill her and slowly took my hands off her mouth.

"He's going to find you and he's going to kill you. Both of you!"
"Who is?" I asked.
"You'll see." She replied insinuating that I wasn't the only one being unfaithful.

She always knew the most devastating ways to hurt me.

"Gut her like the bloated fish she is Candi."
"Grab the bitch's arm!" Candi roared and I did.

As we were about to cut her, Dorothy broke free and bit the tip of Candi's finger off. She made a leap to try and bite at me but I punched her in the face before she could. This knocked her unconscious. Candi was on the ground screaming, bleeding all over the place searching for the rest of her finger.

"Look what you fucking did!" I yelled at my wife. "You dumb bitch!"

Our plan was ruined, there was no way anyone would believe that this was a suicide attempt, not with her face dented in and Candi's DNA in her mouth.

I stripped naked and with the Striphouse steak knife slit my wife's throat from ear to ear. The blood gushed out like a cow at the slaughterhouse.

I sat on the floor still naked, wishing I could kill her again, one more time. I stood up and put the knife back in Dorothy, this time in her stomach.

"That's for Candi's finger you bitch!" I screamed at her knowing Candi could hear me.

I sat on the bed and checked her Facebook. Her status already had six comments.

Did your husband put you up to this? Some asshole wrote.

I told you not to marry him. Her father wrote.

By now Dorothy's phone was ringing nonstop, it was only a matter of time before someone showed up with the police. Candi stood up showing me her found fingertip.

"I have to go the hospital." She said as she sniffed.
"You're going to be fine baby."
"How?" That was the last question she'd ever ask me.

Candi was usually the one comforting me, how the roles had shifted. I kissed her neck and held her warm breasts in my hands.

"Wait here, I'll take care of everything" I told her.

I took the knife out of Dorothy's bulging stomach and blessed myself with it. Candi's DNA was all over the room and Dorothy looked like she had been hit by a bus. There was no other option. I slide the knife gently into Candi's side and twisted it. She took a step back to absorb the wound and fell to her knees. It was always such a beautiful sight watching Candi drop to her knees. I watched her eyes as she slowly died.

It was a much cleaner and sexier job than Dorothy's horror show. I placed Candi's hand on the knife so it looked like a suicide. Afterwards, I took a shower and washed the blood from my naked body. Once clean and

seanie sugrue

dry, I applied some U.A.F to my scalp and combed it in.
I put my suit and scarf back on and said my final
goodbye to Candi. Our beautiful moment was cut short
by the sound of sirens approaching from afar. Before
leaving the room, I slapped my dead wife one more time
and spat on her. I took her keys, stole her faster car and
made my way back to Manhattan.

Two dead dogs, two dead bodies in my fucking bedroom
and I could never fuck Candi again.

"Fucking bitch!" I screamed and started punching the
dashboard.

It wasn't a dream. This was my reality now. I stared
back in the mirror and all I could see was baldness, an
empty scalp, not a hair on my bald fucking head.

Nothing happens on God's earth by mistake.

Mitten text me. I had forgot all about Mitten.

Are you coming to the meeting?

***I've never gone to an AA meeting and not felt better
afterwards.***

I text her back. *On my way. ;)*

It had been months, but I decided it was time to call my
long-lost sponsor. He didn't pick up so I left him a
voicemail.

"Hey David, it's me. I know it's been awhile since I
called you but the truth is that I have felt like you were
beneath me, that I was vastly superior to you and your

family. David, I need some fucking compassion. I want
you to know that you were right. I'm still fucking bald
and I've been combing my bald head for the last six
months trying to convince myself there was something
there. It was out of line for me to be so unfaithful to my
wife, fucking hookers is wrong, you're absolutely
correct. Candi probably only wanted me for my money,
well, Dorothy's money. She caught me cheating so I'd
have been laughed out of the courtroom. I wouldn't have
got shit. I did what I had to do. Anyway, if you agree to
sponsor me again, I'll be better to people going forward,
no more cheating, no more hookers, no underage girls,
no more killing people out of my own selfishness. I'll
take the hidden cameras out of the bathroom at work.
I'm about to catch some of the ten pm meeting, maybe if
you're around try and stop by for a chat? Alright well
look, give me a call back when you get this and we'll
talk about moving forward together. I love you man."

I hung up and felt instant relief. The voicemail went well
and I started to put things into perspective. It was Candi
that killed the dogs and I had to put Dorothy down after
she bit my girls finger off. How could it have ended any
other way? How could I have allowed the love of my life
to go to prison for killing the disgusting mule I married?
I saved Candi and knew it. As for the baldness, perhaps I
hadn't been applying enough *U.A.F.* It was a rough day
but I was sober and as long as I had my sobriety there
was a chance. The health store was still in operation and
Mittens fake tits were divine.

I drove to the East Village, abandoning Dorothy's car
and reality on Avenue D, D for death they say. I got to
the ten pm meeting late but half a meeting is better than
no meeting at all.

I saw Mitten and her fake tits I adored sitting in the same seat that she had been in the night before. Her low-cut top revealed the beginning of her large plastic breasts. Her short black skirt was made from suede with matching army boots. I had spent the entire day obsessing over Candi and Crystal that I'd forgot about Mitten and how she had sucked on my neck like a vacuum only a few hours earlier. Mitten presented herself as a feminist but underneath all that bullshit, she was a dirty little whore like the rest of them and craved my St. Peter. Staring at her tits I felt genuine nirvana and I was as hard as an Eskimo's nipple ring.

She hated how much she needed me.

By now I assumed the cops had discovered my stout orangutan of a wife's body. They would have been investigating the homicide/suicide, wondering what the hell Candi had been thinking and how they could break the news to me. Mitten was sitting in a way that I could see the top of her black padded bra. I couldn't wait to take it off with my teeth later. I'd wear that bra around my head like a madman. I combed my hair and put my hand up.

The speaker called on me to share from the floor. I couldn't think of anything to say that would impress Mitten so I went with the safe option and said the tenth step prayer.

"Dear God, I pray that I may grow in understanding and in effectiveness, to take daily spot check inventories, to correct mistakes when I make them, to take responsibility for my actions, to be ever aware of my negative and self-defeating attitude and behaviors, to keep my willfulness in check, to always remember I need Your help, to keep love and tolerance of others as my code, and to continue in daily prayer how I can best serve You."

I could tell people at the meeting were impressed with citing the prayer word for word, but at the same time they wanted me to share some knowledge from my own experience in the program. I continued.

"A life unexamined isn't a life worth living. You don't believe me? Look around." I pointed to all of the empty seats. "Empty chairs, people dying. I've seen people in halfway houses taken out in cardboard coffins. They just write your initials on the side of it. Today has been a challenging day with a few ups and a few downs, but at the end of it, I'm going to bed sober tonight and nothing is more important than that. We are all blessed to have found these rooms because so many don't. My life used to be a mystery and now because of Alcoholics Anonymous, it's an erotic drama. Thanks for listening."

"Thanks for sharing." The room responded in awe.

Mitten seemed a little detached and played on her cell phone instead of listening to my powerful message. It was only her third day sober and she knew she couldn't have done it without me. She whispered in my ear that she'd be right back and I haven't seen her since. I started questioning my connection with my higher power until the doors swung open and in walked Phil.

God works in mysterious ways.

Phil sat in the back row and immediately nodded off.

After the meeting, I tried to make a dash for the door to find Mitten, but the old bitch sitting behind me asked if I could help Phil.

"He's a lost cause." I told her.
"Can you help me carry him?" she asked.
"Get out of my way."

I picked up Phil over my shoulder and carried him downstairs. Once I got him outside, I shook him and he woke up from his coma.

Out of nowhere, some homeless prick in an *I Love the Bronx* t-shirt sucker punched Phil knocking him to the pavement head first. Mitten wasn't even on the fucking block.

"What the fuck man?" I yelled at the vagrant as he sauntered away.
"What the hell did you do to him?" I asked Phil who was now bleeding on the ground.

What the fuck is going on? I wondered to myself. That's when I got this strange sensation that someone was watching me. My paranoia proved to be legitimate as a dozen cops surrounded me with their guns drawn.

"Look, I sent her that dick pic by mistake, it was for my wife!" I screamed at them. "I already apologized to her!"

A black cop ran towards me and tried to push me to the ground. I picked him up and threw him head first through the side window of a parked taxi. I kicked another one to the ground and started running east. While attempting to jump over a moving car I heard the gunfire. They shot me in the fucking back. As I tried to get up, they kicked the hands out from under me and I fell back to the ground.

I laid there staring at the sky trying to understand what God wanted.

I thought about Crystal and if she would save herself for me and not have sex with her douchebag actor boyfriend. I thought about her birthday party, drinking milk shakes, holding her in my arms and unbuttoning her shirt.

I thought about Candi and the nights we spent together. I thought about her toes that I'd been sucking on, and now she was dead.

I thought about Dorothy and the night we got married. She had told me that she'd love me for the rest of my life. The boisterous donkey.

As I tried to get up from the pool of blood beneath me a cop stood on my fucking neck muttering something about a partner of his.

It's not about the destination, it's about the journey.

I think about what the inside of Mittens bra would have looked like, the padding and the tags. I'd wear her bra on my head like a madman.

I close my eyes.

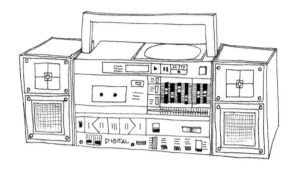

3.

Dorothy

Another morning spent staring at the cracks in the ceiling and the bunions on my feet, waiting for the alarm. I was terrified her husband had harmed her.

Did she mean it when she whispered that she loved me or was it just the wine talking?

The answer wasn't on the ceiling and it didn't appear to be on the floor or on my crooked feet. I checked my phone for the twentieth time and felt sick to my stomach, there was still nothing from her.

I'd ran into my new lady a few months earlier at a Bob Dylan concert in New Jersey. My date had blown me off on short notice. She said that I was incapable of understanding boundaries and at times, would become too controlling. I'm not perfect, but I think controlling was a bit harsh and my lack of boundaries was an exaggeration. I'd spent close to a week's salary on the tickets and was unable to convince anyone to take my now extra one, so the night before the show I sold the ticket on StubHub.

After arriving alone I'd convinced myself that I wouldn't stay for the entire show because it was awkward being there by myself. Then, I heard her voice.

"Are you the StubHub guy?"

She was eloquent and elegant, so graceful. It was love at first sight. I was so in awe of her beauty that I didn't even respond to the question.

"What kind of a loser goes to a Bob Dylan concert alone?" She asked, not acknowledging that she was also by herself.

I said something about how I had to be alone when Bob sang, so I could absorb the lyrics. She offered me one of her two beers and I said that I was driving.

"Me too." She said smiling.
"I'm a cop." I said flashing my detective badge and she appeared ambivalent.
"I'm Dorothy."

I took the beer and we toasted to a great night. The lights went down and Bob walked on stage opening with one of my favorites, *Tambourine Man*. We chatted in between songs and she told me that she wished her grandfather could have been there. I didn't ask, but I assumed he was a huge Dylan fan and probably dead. We walked out of the arena together after the show.

"Where are you parked?" I asked.
"I took the train."
"So, you lied to me?"

She smiled and turned around, taking far too many steps away from me. I stood still under the streetlamp watching her, not knowing what to say or how to get her to come back.

"Would you like a ride home?" I yelled behind her.
"You live in Yonkers." She said, looking straight through me with her unforgettable blue eyes.
"Queens is practically on the way." It was far from.

My car was a mess. There were about a dozen Bob Dylan CD's on the passenger seat, wrappers and empty coke bottles spread across the floor. She looked through my CD collection and made fun of me for owning Dylan's greatest hits. Apparently, that exempted me from calling myself a true fan. I told her it was a gift and she laughed.

"What's your favorite album?" She asked.
"Freewheelin'."
"Exempt!" She reiterated.

Before I could fire the question back, she said *Blood on the Tracks* and put it on. By the time we got to her house *Shelter from the Storm* was playing and it was fittingly pouring rain outside. Neither of us had an umbrella so we agreed that she should just wait in the car until the storm faded. She owned a real estate company but didn't spend a lot of time there. The company ran itself so she had more free time than she'd like. Her new passion was bowling and she played on a team every Tuesday night. I hadn't bowled in years but joked that I'd be willing to give her a free lesson. Although the conversation seemed to be going well, in my mind I was trying to find the right time to make a move and kiss her. I wasn't sure if I was misreading the signs or if she actually liked me. After the incredible evening we had I didn't want to ruin it by coming off as some kind of creep.

We had been parked outside her house chatting for two hours.

"I should go." She said.
"Yeah, I'm sorry."
"Why?"

I wasn't sure, it was just something I'd say. It was an anxiety thing. She took my phone from the dashboard and put her number in it.

"Thanks." That was just something I'd say too. It was a joyful thing.

She had bowling practice the following night and told me if I was feeling up for it to tag along. I didn't want to sound overly enthusiastic or desperate so I said I'd see how I was feeling. I wasn't sure if she meant it as a date, but I couldn't take the smile off of my face. As she was getting out of the car I yelled after her.

"Wait!"
"For what?" She asked.
"How am I supposed to call you?" I said picking up her phone from the seat.

She put her left knee on the passenger seat and kissed me on the lips. As she leaned back, I tried to kiss her one more time, but my seat belt pulled me back. She smiled at me before closing the door. She ran to the house with her long brown hair getting soaked in the rain. When she got to her porch, she took a couple of steps towards the door before looking right back at me. She smiled again before walking inside her house.

Life is a different experience when you're in love. It changes your entire attitude, you stop seeing the negative in everything and start focusing more on the good. However, my experience with love is that it rarely comes without complication.

Less than a month later I was staring at the ceiling looking for answers, wondering if I should have the bunion on my right foot removed by a surgeon. I thought about the food in the fridge and wondered if it was still good.

The night after the concert I bowled a forty-six and her friends found my lack of talent hilarious.

"Where the hell did you find him?" One of her teammates asked and the rest of the team laughed, not her though.

I bought the whole team a round of beers and they seemed to forget about my embarrassing performance. Her friend had an unpaid public urination ticket and I gave him advice on how to go about paying it.

After all her friends left, we stayed and grabbed another drink at the bar. She asked me about my job and if I enjoyed being a detective.

"Some days are better than others." I said.

On our third date we went to her favorite Chinese restaurant. The interior wasn't anything special but she insisted that their food was the best. Regardless of the casualness of the restaurant, Dorothy wore a long black dress with pearls. She looked incredible. I was astonished when she told me that she was thirty-seven. I hadn't asked, but assumed she was in her mid-twenties. One thing I've learned from dating thirty something year old's is to prepare yourself for the, there's something I have to tell you.

"There's something I have to tell you." She said after we ordered our appetizers.
"Okay." Bracing myself.
"I have two kids."

I was relieved at first. I'd never had any of my own so I cherished the idea of being a father figure to these two kids. After the waiter brought us our main course, she told me that there was a detail she left out. The kids had a father.

"But you're not with him anymore, right?"
"Technically I am."
"But you're going to leave him?"
"It's not that easy."

They hadn't signed a prenuptial agreement and if she filed for divorce then he would take half of the inheritance. Her grandfather recently died and had left her millions in his will. It wasn't that she was worried about losing the money, but more that she didn't want him to have it.

She had been suspicious for some time that he'd been cheating on her and insisted that it was only a matter of time before he slipped up. I suggested that she should hire a private detective to follow him and we agreed that she would look into it.

After we finished our food, we went for a walk-through Greenwich Village. Holding hands, we strolled through Washington Square Park and sat by the fountain. A man nearby was playing Beatles songs on his guitar and Dorothy yelled at him to play some Dylan. He played *Like a Rolling Stone* and we danced and kissed under the stars.

The weeks following, I had constant battles with my conscience. I was once on the receiving end of a secret romance when my ex-wife cheated on me. Now I was the other man and it had me wrestling with my morals. Last night we went back to our Chinese spot and when we pulled up outside her house, she could tell I was upset.

"What's wrong?"
"You know what's wrong."
"Mitten is coming by with evidence tomorrow." She said. "It's almost over."

Mitten was her private detective. She promised to bring the proof Dorothy needed the following day.

"Will you meet me in the morning?" She asked.

For the last two weeks I had been stopping by her house before work after her husband left. It wasn't ideal, but I appreciated any time I could spend with her.

As she got out of the car she turned around.

"I love you."

She closed the door before I could respond.

"I love you too." I cooed to the closed door.

At two am Dorothy emailed me saying that she and her husband had been in a fight and he had thrown a wine bottle at her, but insisted that she was okay. I'd have loved to spend the entire day at her house consoling her, but this visit was going to be a short one.

The East Village had become a war zone. Bunny Goodstuff was flooding the streets with heroin and the idea of having a serial killer at large was becoming more of a possibility with the latest disappearances. On my way to Dorothy's I text my partner Max.

I'm going to be a little late. Cover me.

I parked my unmarked police car outside while I waited for her demented husband to leave. After about five minutes he walked out of their house wearing a suit with a skinny purple scarf. The sun bounced off his bald head as he went to his car. He was 6'3" and at least three hundred pounds, but my money was on Max if they ever came to blows. We nicknamed Dorothy's husband Juicy because of his obvious steroid use.

Dorothy had given me a spare set of keys to the house at our restaurant the night before, an attempt to validate our relationship.

After allowing myself in, I was greeted by a smiling Dorothy in the vestibule holding her loving arms out for me. I looked at her and she stared back at me while undoing her sherbet orange robe. I wondered if I'd ever leave that house again. After making love I went to the kitchen and made us a pot of coffee.

"Ditch work and hang out with me all day." She requested.
"I wish." I thought about calling the sergeant right then and there to quit.

Before leaving I noticed the smashed bottle of wine still on the floor in the kitchen, a reminder of the dangerous situation she was still in. She assured me that it was only a matter of minutes before her private detective would deliver substantial evidence to present to the judge. Then, we would spend the rest of our lives together.

As I walked out of the house she ran after me dressed again in her robe and slippers.

"Wait!"
I waited.
"How about I stay with you tonight?"
"Your husband?"
"I don't care." She said.
"I'll pick you up around ten?"

Six women and a man had been reported missing over the last three months. The latest was a girl named Susie Jones and her boyfriend Quincy Quinn.

Susie was an East Village native who just so happened to work at Dorothy's husbands' store in Astoria. I couldn't help but ask myself if it was just a coincidence. Regardless of his potential participation in the disappearances, my main objective was to get Dorothy out of that house as quick as possible.

We had pounds of heroin coming into the East Village every day. Bunny Goodstuff had earned her nickname as The Drug Lord of Tompkins Square Park.

"She's a midget selling drugs in the park!" Sergeant Bigley would scream. "She fucking stands out!"

Sergeant Bigley was white trash from Woodlawn, an Irish stronghold in the Bronx and a third-generation cop. Despite having three young kids at home, he drank most nights at a nearby Irish bar. Bigley had it out for my partner Max.

Max was like a brother to me. He grew up in the roughest part of Staten Island and carried a giant chip on his shoulder. I was excited when he got to meet Dorothy, we took him and a girl he was seeing to the bowling alley. Max rolled a one sixty but insisted that he hadn't played before. I finished last again rolling a fifty-two. He was an incredible cop but sometimes let his temper get the better of him.

I arrived at the ninth precinct at 10:30 am, almost two hours late and was greeted by Bigley.

"What the fuck, you stupid fucking..." He yelled, restraining himself from saying something he'd later regret.
"I'm not your wife and kids, don't yell at me."

This threw him off and he struggled to find his words.

"What fucking time do you call this?!" He yelled while munching on a pastry.
"Ten thirty." I responded contemptuously. "I've been working all night."

"You better bring that little midget bitch in here today or you and Max will be handing out parking tickets!" He yelled spitting vanilla icing in my face.

He was referring to Bunny Goodstuff and as much as I didn't want to admit it, he was right. It was time to bring her in.

I sat at my desk thinking about Dorothy, hoping Mitten would get us out of this mess. I updated my Facebook profile picture to the one she took of me at the bowling alley on our second date with the caption *the second-best night of my life,* and it was. I'd already told her that the Bob Dylan concert in New Jersey was number one.

While waiting for Dorothy to validate the photograph, I felt a double tap on my back and knew it was Max. We hugged. A lot of the guys at the precinct would break our balls, but they were jealous of our brotherhood.

"Max, why are you holding a boombox?"
"I need you to trust me. Say it"
"Say what?'
"That you trust me."
"I trust you."

He nodded his head.

"We go to the park, take off our shirts and act like a couple of drug dealers. Bunny Goodstuff isn't going to like two black guys dealing drugs in her territory."

Bunny was incredibly racist and notoriously territorial. The brilliant part was that the boombox was also a tape recorder. Max had been hitting the gym more than me, so the taking the shirts off part wasn't particularly appealing, but I agreed to go along with it.

"Can we get breakfast first?"

We arrived at *Rock Bottom* diner on Astor Place a little before noon. I told Max about the broken wine bottle in Dorothy's kitchen.

"Let me take care of this guy." Max pleaded.

Dorothy had asked me not to get involved, saying that she had it under control. As much as it hurt, I respected her requisitions. Max and I spoke about the potential serial killer and the seven people that had gone missing. He asked if I thought Juicy had any part to play in the disappearance of Susie Jones.

"The guy is a menace Max, but I don't think he's murdering people."

Dorothy was calling so I went outside to take the call.

"Everything okay?"
"He's out banging hookers every night."

Thank God for Mitten.

"Change your locks and I'll see you soon." I told her.

I went back in the diner grinning from ear to ear.

"What are you so happy about?" Max asked.
"Breakfast is on me."

As I was bringing Max up to speed Billy Bigley called.
We flipped a coin to see who had to answer it.

"Tails never fails." Max said before he lost.
"What?!" Max answered causing me to laugh.
Max's face dropped and he put the phone on the table.
"Jesus fucking Christ."

They found two corpses on Randall's Island, one male
and one female, neither had their head attached. It was
believed to be Susie Jones and her boyfriend Quincy
Quinn.

Jesus fucking Christ was right.

The August sun hadn't been kind to either of them. The
insects, rats and birds had already eaten off most of their
flesh.

"Good God." Max said.
"God had nothing to do with this."

Susie's shorts were around what was left of her ankles
and Quincy was wearing nothing but a wrist watch. That
was when I got the notification that Dorothy had liked
my Facebook profile picture. I showed the notification to
Max and he nodded his head as if to say I told you so.
Quincy Quinn was holding a sports bra in his right hand.
It was beginning to fade but we could still see the *House
of Gains* logo written across the front. It was Susie Jones
alright.

"Why do you think they took the heads? I asked Max.
"Human beings are fucked up." He said.

We got back inside our car and sat for a moment in an attempt to refocus our minds. Max broke the silence.

"Maybe we should take a trip over there?"
"Over where?

When we arrived at *House of Gains,* we were greeted by a young girl wearing an outfit resembling a Hooters uniform, but seedier. Her name was Crystal, the new assistant manager. We flashed our badges and asked if she didn't mind answering some questions about Susie Jones. She told us that some creep had been coming to the store dressed in different costumes and took special interest in Susie.

"What kind of costumes?" I asked.
"Different personas." She said. "A garbage man once, a male nurse another time."

While we were taking down the character description of the creep, Crystal received a text message and shook her head in disgust.

"The disgusting prick." She said to herself.
"Everything okay?" I asked.
"Look, can I tell you guys something, off the record?"

Max and I looked at one another. We both nodded our heads.

Crystal told us that the owner was paying Susie fifteen hundred dollars each time they fucked. She quit because she didn't need the money anymore.

Had she vanished without a trace because he couldn't risk Dorothy finding out about their expensive affair?

Dorothy called me again on our way back to the car. She told me with everything going on it would be best if we waited until the following day to see each other. I was upset that she was cancelling on me, but it was with good reason.

If I'd known that was the last time I would ever talk to Dorothy I'd have said so much more. I'd have told her that she was all I ever needed, that her soul existing was the sugar in my coffee. The jam on my toast.

"Let's go get Bunny Goodstuff." Max said.

We realized during our commute to Tompkins Square Park that we didn't have anything to play on the boombox, so we stopped by *Kim's Music Store* and bought a CD. Max wasn't a Dylan fan so we compromised and picked out a Biggie Smalls CD, *It Was All a Dream*. We didn't realize it at the time, but the CD we bought was a single, not a full album. We had to listen to the same song on repeat for the rest of the afternoon.

We took our shirts off and blasted Biggie as loud as the boombox would go. It only took five minutes before we had our first junkie looking to score. He was a skinny white kid who smelled like he hadn't showered in weeks.

"Cut the shit, I have forty bucks and I want a bag of the good stuff." He demanded.

Max winked at me nodding his head as if to say I told you so. The kid was a dumpster fire and we knew his condition was the work of the hateful Bunny Goodstuff.

"You think we're dealers because we're black?" Max asked.

The kid responded with a racist remark and Max pushed him to the ground. He put him in a headlock for a few seconds before I could break it up. The kid ran off after I separated them. Max was a hot head, this wasn't unusual.

"What the fuck Max?!"
"That little bitch thought we were dealers."
"That was the idea."

Max knew he messed up, but I wasn't going to grill him all day over it. We put the music back on but no one else approached us. A while later we received a disturbance call from a nearby drinking establishment called *The Pine Box*. This sort of thing usually wouldn't interest us, and it didn't, until we heard the culprit's description, a midget in a baby blue pillowcase. We put our shirts back on, hid the boombox behind a tree and headed to St. Mark's Place.

A young white woman was sitting in the back of an ambulance with her top lip hanging off like a caterpillar and a dent on her head the size of a tennis ball. Bunny Goodstuff was already gone.

"I get that you're in a lot of pain but can I ask you a couple of questions?" Max asked.

The paramedic told us that the victim was in no state for questioning and I agreed. Max demanded that he respect our interrogation and I had to hold him back for the second time.

cardboard coffins

"Where is she? Where is Goodstuff!" Max yelled.

The sight of the two rotten beheaded corpses had impaired his judgement. I sat him down on the nearby stoop before thanking the paramedic for all that he did. Max lit a cigarette as he watched the ambulance drive away.

"I was trying to find out what happened." He said.
"You said you quit smoking."
"Leave me the fuck alone."

While we were on the stoop arguing, a young man came marching towards us muttering nonsense about his predicament.

"Come here now a second, I've no fucking notion what the story was with that runt, but it had fuck all to do with me."

Unlike Billy Bigley, this guy was off the boat from Ireland and at first Max and I didn't have any idea what he was trying to say.

"You work here?" I asked.
"What kind of stupid fucking question is that?" He asked pointing to *The Pine Box* polo shirt.
"We are going to need a statement from you." I said.
"No fucking danger I'm giving you anything."
"He wasn't asking for permission." Max said.

His name was Jimmie and he had been cheating on his wife with the girl from the back of the ambulance. Not only was he married, but he also had a newborn baby at home.

"Who the hell do you think you are?" I asked him. "You think you can do whatever you want?"
"There's no law against cheating." He said.

We watched the footage downstairs with the disloyal bartender. The assault was vicious. Bunny entered the establishment with some individual that Jimmie invited into the kitchen. Bunny sat alone in the corner.

"Who is he?" I asked.
"No idea." Jimmie responded.
"Don't fucking lie to him." Max said.
"I'm not lying."
"Then what was he doing in the fucking kitchen?" Max asked.
"He was in here a few nights ago and forgot to pay. I didn't want to embarrass him in front of his runt."

For some reason we believed him.

The girl from the ambulance was sitting next to Bunny drinking red wine. The situation escalated quickly from a conversation into a hellacious one-sided assault. Bunny smashed her wine glass and used an ashtray like a baseball bat, smashing it across her face.

"Why the fuck do you have ashtrays on the bar?" Max asked Jimmie. "You can't smoke in here."
"It looks cool."
That's when I noticed who the guy in the kitchen was.
"Wait, rewind the tape." I said.

Jimmie rewound the tape.

"You have ashtrays on the bar because it looks cool?" Max asked again.

"It gives the place a feeling of authenticity."
"Press pause!"

It was him, the junkie from the park that asked for the good stuff. Max grabbed Jimmie and put him up against the wall.

"Who the fuck is he?!"
"I've no fucking idea who that fella is." Jimmie pleaded.
"How about I call your wife right now and tell her what you've been up to?" I warned.
"You wouldn't." Jimmie pleaded.
"Wouldn't I?"
Max tightened his grip.
"His name is Phil." Jimmie confessed. "He comes in here sometimes, but that's all I know about him."

For some reason we believed him.

"Fancy a drink?" Max asked.

We hung out at the bar and watched a few innings of the Mets game. Max ordered a plate of nachos and a beer. I had a chicken salad and a sparkling water. Jimmie told us everything was on the house so Max ordered two more beers. Sometime during the sixth inning we decided it was time to get back to work. As we stood up to leave, I noticed Jimmie was in the kitchen with another woman. We could only see the back of her head, but figured she was another twenty something year old he was messing around with.

"How the hell do people live like that?" I asked Max before picking up our twenty-dollar tip from the bar.

On our way back to the park, I finally said what had
been on both our minds all day.

"Max, didn't those bodies remind you a lot..."
"...Don't fucking say it!" Max shouted interrupting me.
"All I'm saying is…" Max interrupted me again.
"…He's dead."
"Is he?"

After we were assigned to work together, one of our first
assignments was hunting and investigating the Chef,
Tommy Fogarty. Tommy was a serial killer who savored
the taste of human flesh. He was born and raised on
Fordham Road and got the name Chef because of his
unique ability to cook human meat. Chef was a popular
guy around his neighborhood, notorious for his copious
displays of generosity. So generous in fact that he would
bring a homemade pot of soup to the nearby homeless
shelter every Sunday. Tommy's charity came with
deadly consequences.

One weekend a number of the shelter's residents fell ill.
They all contracted the same virus, one that you could
only obtain from consuming human meat. Not only was
Tommy murdering and eating his victims, he was
feeding them to the whole Goddamn neighborhood. On
top of the meat, he would cut out the victim's vital
organs and mail them to their nearest and dearest in a
cardboard box. On Christmas Eve 2010, Jeff Morgan
took his own life after he received a package with his
daughter's heart in it. The card simply stated, *thank you*.
When we finally tracked him down and broke into his
house all that we found in his fridge were three human
heads.

Max and I were cooking mac n' cheese with fancy bacon when we got the call in the spring of 2015. Chef had broken out of Rikers. He was presumed dead, but his body was never found.

As we got closer to the park, we heard our anthem *It Was All a Dream* blaring from the boombox. We looked at one another confused and ran towards the tree where we had left it.

A homeless man wearing an *I Love the Bronx* t-shirt was using the boombox as a toy, dancing around the park like a lunatic. Max pushed him to the ground.

"You think you're funny or something? He yelled as he put him in his infamous headlock.
"Max stop!"

After he released him, Max kicked the homeless man up the ass before he could run out of the park.

"You're no better than him right now!" I screamed.
"Fuck you!" He yelled back. "It's called retaliation."
"Does that make you feel better?"
"Yeah, it does."
"Just another violent cop abusing his authority." I said.

He sat silently on one bench and I sat on the other. During our muteness, I decided to give Dorothy a call. For reasons unknown to me at the time she didn't pick up, then Max broke the silence.

"Check your Facebook!"

The first thing that showed up in my news feed was Dorothy's status, a suicide note.

Hey guys, I love all of you and I think you all love me too. However, this crazy world has gotten too wacky for me and I can't go on. My beautiful husband, this isn't your fault, you're the only reason I've lasted as long as I have. I love you.

I responded to her Facebook status

Did your husband put you up to this?

"There's another." Max said.

And I'm taking the dogs with me.

Jesus fucking Christ.

"He's at the fucking house!" Max screamed and we both sprinted to our car.

First, he decapitated Susie Jones and Quincy Quinn, now Dorothy was next. Max was right. How could I have been too naive to see it? I was too busy blaming a dead man.

The GPS said it would take us forty minutes to get to Forest Hills, but Max got us there in twenty-six. He bumped a guy off of his bike coming off the 59th Street bridge and I reiterated how he shouldn't have drunk all those beers. We didn't have time to stop, but in Max's defense the cyclist could have made more of an effort to get out of the way.

Several police cars were already parked in front of her house. It was a Goddamn crime scene. Max told me to wait outside. I feared for the worst. I sat on the hood of the car and watched Max enter the house. Hardly a minute had passed when he came back out looking like he'd seen a ghost, maybe he had.

"Don't go in there" He said.
"What's going on?"
"It's fucked up in there."
"Max?"
"They're both dead."
"They?"

Max made little effort to try and stop me from going inside. We walked up the stairs together and into the bedroom. Dorothy was lying in a pool of blood on the bed, her throat sliced open and face battered so badly that I wouldn't have recognized her if not for the sherbet robe. It didn't take a detective to know that this wasn't a suicide.

"Everyone get the hell out of here." I yelled.

They all left, except Max.

"We're too late." I said. "Who the fuck is she?"

Another woman in a short red dress was lying dead on the floor by the end of the bed. She had a rose tattoo on her thigh and the knife was still stuck in her chest. The tip of her right index finger was missing.

"What kind of an animal did this?" Max asked.
"A bald animal, with a skinny scarf."

I sat on the bed beside Dorothy and kissed her on the forehead. My hands shook as I wiped the blood from her cheek. I put my two arms around her shoulders and pulled her as close to me as I could. I could never get close enough to her. She was staring at me with her two sad dead eyes. I closed them with my fingers and told her that I'd love her forever.

Max was on the floor going through the other victims' belongings. While I was ordering the forensics team to treat Dorothy with respect Max let out a sigh.

"What's wrong Max?"
"Nothing." He responded before leaving the room.

I could tell that Max had found something in her purse, so I followed him. On our way out of the house I got on my knees in the vestibule where Dorothy and I had been making love that morning. Max kneeled next to me and handed me what he found in the purse.

It was Mitten's business card, Dorothy's private detective.

"Why the fuck does she have that?" I asked.
Max shrugged his shoulders.
"And why would he post a fucking suicide note and then do that?" I asked Max.
"Something went wrong." He said. "She fought back,"

I looked around the room and noticed the wine bottle was still smashed in the corner, it hit me.
"Max, I know where he is."

Dorothy told me once that he hadn't missed his ten pm AA meeting in years. Max put his foot down and we were back in the East Village in twenty minutes, flat.

During the commute we got a report stating that another employee from the *House of Gains* store had been reported missing. Tammy Stone, a former Miss Teen Arizona missed an audition and didn't show up to work. As we pulled up on Houston Street, Billy Bigley and a dozen other officers were already standing outside the meeting.

The bald fuckers former sponsor had called in reporting that he admitted to murdering his wife in a voicemail and was in route to the meeting. Bigley knew I was emotionally invested and warned me not to do anything drastic.

"Don't fucking shoot him, we have to bring him in alive." Billy urged.

The meeting wasn't going to end until 11:15 pm and out of respect to their anonymity, Bigley made us wait outside until it concluded. We both knew the real reason we lingered, because the Sergeant had a drinking problem and he didn't want to risk relating to something he heard.

Max leaned against the car and smoked another cigarette. It was only beginning to set in, Dorothy was dead. Only a few hours earlier she was telling me how she loved me, that she wanted to spend the rest of her life with me and now she was dead. I closed my eyes and could still feel her breathing, could still see her smile painted across her glorious face, the light reflecting in her blue eyes.

The meeting ended and the crowd started to disburse. Max was nowhere to be seen.

"Have you seen Max?" I asked Bigley.

He hadn't.

The bald fucker with a skinny scarf walked outside. He was carrying Phil the junkie who looked even worse than he had before.

"I know that kid." I said to Bigley.

Out of nowhere the homeless man in the *I Love the Bronx* t-shirt came up behind them and sucker punched Phil the junkie.

"What the fuck is going on?" I said to Bigley. "I know him too."

The homeless man bolted and Phil stumbled after him. Only the bald fucker with a skinny scarf remained. He slowly looked left and then to the right. He knew we were there, and he knew we knew he knew that we were there. He started running down Houston Street and we chased him. As I tried to tackle him, he picked me up by the ears and threw me head first through the side window of a parked car. Bigley attempted to bring him down but like me, was sent flying through the air. While trying to climb out the window of the yellow taxi I heard it, like a roll of thunder.

CRACK CRACK!!

My eardrums rang. Max was standing over the bald fucker who was still wearing the skinny scarf. He pointed his gun at his bald head.

"Don't fucking shoot him again!" Billy Bigley yelled from the ground holding his busted foot.

There was another girl missing and the only person that knew anything about her whereabouts was lying on the sidewalk under Max. We needed to bring him in alive.

"Max don't do it!" I screamed, but already knew it was too late. Max had made up his mind.

CRACK!

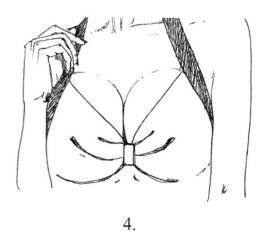

4.

Mitten

I woke up to a cab driver yelling on the corner of 29th Street and 2nd Avenue.

"Lady, you're here!"

It read 5:55 am on his clock. I was home.

Once inside I plugged in my phone and fed Ginger and Muddy before it powered back on. There were seven text messages and one new voicemail. Six of the texts were from Dorothy and the other from Quincy's mom. Each of Dorothy's texts read *blah blah blah* and Quincy's mom didn't offer any worthwhile information either. The voicemail from Phil was common, yet concerning.

"Mitten, I love you Mitten, but I can't do it anymore. I love you Mitten."

It was obvious from his slurring and repetition that he was wasted again. I tried to call him back but he didn't pick up. I could only hope that he was somewhere safe and sleeping it off. I set an alarm for seven so I could get to Dorothy's house by eight. The now nourished kittens jumped on top of me and we fell asleep.

I was juggling two different cases at the same time. Not only was Dorothy's abusive and loveless marriage doomed to fail, but she also suspected that he was being unfaithful. Her family had more money than the Queen of England and her husband was a manipulative deadbeat that somehow convinced her that a prenup was unwarranted. If Dorothy filed for divorce without evidence of his frequent infidelity he would have been entitled to half of her fortune. If she could somehow get her paws on a picture of him screwing around, that would be greeted with a very different reaction in the courtroom. That's where I came in.

The flat rate for my surveillance was usually two hundred dollars an hour, but I charged Dorothy three hundred after becoming aware of her wealth. One of the first things I discovered about her creep of a husband was that he was a member of Alcoholics Anonymous. Despite it being an anonymous program, he posted a daily progress report on Facebook.

2,816 days sober and I'm feeling fine. Find your own concept of God. It could be nature or a star in the sky. ;)

2,822 days sober and despite having negative people in my life, I remain positive and grateful. ;)

2,825 days sober and some people need to work on their judgmental nature. When you point your finger at me

*you have three more pointing back at you, four if you're
double jointed. ;)*

He ran an unsuccessful business called *House of Gains*
which specialized in getting meatheads over the counter
legal and illegal steroids. All his staff were young girls
aged somewhere between sixteen and twenty-two. The
uniform was a sports bra and extra short shorts. One of
his newer employees Tammy told me that he weighed
each girl before their shift and would threaten to suspend
or replace them if they didn't make weight.

I met him on my second trip to the store. He was
screaming over the counter at one of the girls because of
her lack of enthusiasm. As the girl was about to assist
me, he pushed her out of the way insisting that he had it
under control.

"What can I help you with angel?"

I asked if he could recommend a remedy for my constant
hangovers. He would later refer to this as serendipity.

"There's no magic potions for that babe." He explained.
"The only cure is complete abstinence."
"That doesn't sound feasible."
"What if I told you it is?"
"I'm listening." I said.
"Don't fuck anything up!" He screamed at the girl again.

He put his hand on my lower back and told me to follow
him.

We went to his office in the back room, there were
posters of topless women stuck to the walls and multiple
signs warning the staff that any type of robbery would

not be tolerated. He started promoting his anonymous program in agonizing detail.

"I was a skeptic too darling, but AA is the greatest thing that ever happened to me."

I wondered where he ranked his wife and kids.

We arranged to meet at his regular ten pm meeting that same night. Of course, I didn't have any intention of attending. I waited outside the meeting in my car and took pictures of him leaving with who I would later learn to be his favorite prostitute, Candi. I followed them on foot snapping more pictures of them entering a hotel on St. Mark's Place. The hotel was next door to my ex-boyfriend's bar so I had to be subtle.

I anticipated that the pictures would have been sufficient material for Dorothy to bring to court, but I decided to wait a few days before presenting them. She paid by the hour and had a seemingly endless supply of funds plus, I found Candi intriguing.

I'd been in a complicated relationship for most of the previous year with a guy I'd met back in 2011. After an amazing six months together, he gave me an ultimatum, my brother Phil or him. We broke up and I moved out that same night.

Perhaps it was misdirected heartbreak, but I became obsessed with Candi. The following night I tracked them at the hotel again. A couple of hours later Candi left alone and I followed her on foot from the East Village to the Lower East Side. She stopped off at a dive bar on Ludlow Street and against my better judgement, I followed her inside. After an hour or so of drinking alone I got the courage to send her a drink. Candi walked across the bar and sat next to me. She was wearing a short blue leather dress revealing a rose tattoo on her thigh.

"I heard you bought me a drink?"
"I did."
"What do you want?"
"I wanted to say hello."
"Why?"
"I was thinking we could hang out."
"Are you a fucking cop?"
"No."
"If I fucked your husband you can go fuck yourself!"
"I'm not married."

Candi took my arm and dragged me to the restroom, forcing me to strip to my underwear to prove I wasn't wearing a wire. She was as paranoid as she was beautiful.

"What the fuck do you want?" She asked.
"I was thinking we could hang out."
 "Why does a girl like you need to pay for sex?"
"Why does a girl like you need to sell it?"

On our way out of the bar Candi yelled to the bartender,

"I'll pay you whenever, not now though!"

We walked back to her apartment. She smoked at least two cigarettes during our seven-minute commute.

"You're going to give yourself emphysema." I said.
"Shut your mouth."

seanie sugrue

Ronnie the doorman was sleeping so we operated the elevator ourselves. She lived alone in an apartment four times the size of mine. The building seemed new but the elevator was old, operated with an old rusted handle. I leaned against the back wall and watched Candi operate it. I could tell she was staring at me so I nervously looked at her shoes.

The first thing I noticed when we walked inside was that she had a signed Mick Jagger pop art print on the wall and a Shapiro sculpture sitting on the floor. The surveillance industry clearly wasn't the only one thriving.

"Where did you get that?"
"Mick gave it to me." She responded. "Do you want a drink?"

Candi returned from the kitchen with a bottle of Absolut Citron and two rocks glasses. She kicked off her high heels and sat next to me on the couch. I could feel the perspiration dripping down my forehead as she filled the two glasses to the top with vodka.

"So." She said.
"So." I responded. "What do we do now?"

Candi took a sip of vodka from the bottle, not the glass she poured. She ripped off my shirt and slapped me across the face with it. Before I could complain, she took off her own and glanced toward the bedroom. I followed her leaving the two glasses of vodka behind.

Candi was still lying naked beside me when I woke up the following morning. I got out of bed and checked my phone in the living room. There was a text from Phil

saying he was going to jump off the Triboro Bridge.
That was the third time that week he'd sent me
something in that same region of threat. A few minutes
later Candi entered looking as if she'd walked off a
Victoria's Secret catalog, now wearing sexy lingerie. She
drank both glasses of vodka and poured herself another.

"Aren't you in AA?" I asked her.
"How would you know what I'm in?"

This took me by surprise.

"I saw you there once." I said panicking.
"And what the fuck were you doing there?"
"I was with my brother." I lied again.
"I go there to pick up clients." She said. "Sober people
finish faster and people at bars annoy me."
"We met at a bar."
"Exactly."

Candi sat beside me and lit a cigarette. I put my arm
around her trying to give her a kiss. She elbowed me in
the side nearly knocking me off the couch.

"My flat rate is $2,500 a night, but since we only fucked
around for an hour or two, let's call it two grand."

Her business was flourishing alright.

"Are you kidding me?" I asked her. "I thought we were
having a good time?"
"All my clients have a good time, Mitten."

At least she remembered my name.

We walked to a bank on Delancey Street. She waited outside in the rain smoking another cigarette while I withdrew the cash.

"I need to take out two grand in cash." I said to the banker.
"What do you need that for?" He responded invasively.
"I wasn't aware an explanation was required."
"Just making small talk." He said. "How would you like your bills?"
"I don't care."

While the awkward banker counted the cash, he kept looking over my right shoulder. After the fourth or fifth time I looked back and saw Candi staring in. Her breasts were pressed up against the wet glass and her half-closed black raincoat made it seem like she wasn't wearing anything underneath. Her six-inch-high heels made her look over six-feet-tall and her black sunglasses covered most of her face, making her even more mysterious. She started banging on the window implying that I or the awkward banker needed to hurry up.

"She's pretty isn't she?" I said.

The awkward banker handed me the cash evading the question. When I handed Candi the envelope of cash, she blew smoke in my face muttering something I couldn't understand.

"You know there's nothing sexy about lung cancer."

She stuffed the cash in her purse.

"Pleasure doing business with you, Mitten."
"Now what? I asked.

"Who said there was going to be a now?"

I was about to tell her to fuck off. I really was.

"You want to get breakfast?" She asked.
"Fine, but you're paying."

We went to Candi's favorite diner on Clinton Street and ordered two large plates of blueberry pancakes. She poured a full pot of maple syrup over hers and ordered a second strawberry milkshake as soon as the first came out.

"How do you stay in shape?" I asked.

She drank the last of the syrup out of the pot.

"You're much cuter when you don't talk Mitten."

After breakfast Candi switched seats and we started making out in the booth. A minute or two and a lot of stares later she told me that she never wanted to see or hear from me again. She stood up leaving me in total awe of her. After Candi walked outside, leaving me with the bill, my phone rang.

Mary Quinn's son Quincy had gone missing along with his girlfriend Susie Jones. Coincidentally, Susie worked for Dorothy's slime bag husband at the infamous *House of Gains*. Quincy and Susie were last seen walking down Ditmars Boulevard after she finished her shift at the store.

I decided it was time to close Dorothy's case so I could focus primarily on Quincy. I stopped by her house in Queens and noticed a man that wasn't her husband running out of her house. Once he was gone, I gave Dorothy the pictures from the hotel and was disappointed by her reaction.

"What's this?" She asked.
"Your husband with another woman outside a hotel."
"And this?"
"Your husband with another woman entering the hotel."
"It's not enough."

I respectfully disagreed with her.

"Judges don't give a fuck about possibilities, they want concrete facts." She said. "Either catch him in the act or I'll find another PI that can."

I told her I'd be back the following morning with something more concrete. The idea of having to watch Candi give herself to that slime bag was too much so I went with a more unconventional approach.

I arrived at his meeting at ten pm and the creep recognized me immediately.

"I'm sorry it took me so long." I said.
"It's okay babe, you got here when you were ready."

A few minutes in he placed his hand on the inside of my leg and left it there for the duration of the meeting. He raised his hand and proceeded with his presentation. In breach of the group's traditions, I recorded the entire rant for evidence.

"It's not a chore for me to be here tonight, it's not about a destination and it's not a ritual to me, this is life. Look around. Everyone in this room look around. You see the empty seats? There's a reason they're empty. They aren't all at a Goddamn carnival I'll tell you that much. Empty chairs and people dying. I'm here tonight because I want to get fucking high guys and I don't mean I want to say hello."

My assumption was that he was attempting to tell a joke, but I wasn't certain.

"No, he does not!" The annoying woman behind me yelled
"Am I looking for perfection?"
"No." The woman yelled.
"Am I a saint?" He asked.
"No." She responded once more and this time I agreed with her.
"I'm here to help you help me, I'm here because the only way for me to keep this, is by giving it away to you, I'm here for us."

He continued rambling for another five minutes despite the time limit only being three. After the meeting ended, he asked me if I wanted to grab coffee. I'd arranged in advance for my photographer Bunny to be on location. Arriving at the coffee shop on MacDougal street, we sat in the front patio where I knew Bunny could get a good shot of us. I grew up in New York City so it takes a lot to shock me, but when he started adjusting his bald head with a comb, I was genuinely dumbfounded.

"Have you ever been married?" I asked.
"No, never."
"Kids?"
"No, unfortunately it took till now to find the right woman." He said following with a creepy smile.

By the time the waiter brought us our coffee I couldn't take him any longer. I grabbed his shirt and we started making out. Bunny had mistakenly left the flash on, but he was too distracted to notice. He was also unaware of the hickey I left on the side of his neck.

"How about we get a hotel room gorgeous"' He asked.
"I really like you." I told him. "But I can't tonight."
"I'm scared too." He said.

I stood up getting ready to leave and then he added more.

"I'd never hurt you Mitten." He promised. "But this sexual tension needs to be addressed."
"I'll see you tomorrow night."
"Let's at least go to the bathroom so I can get a look at your pussy." He insisted.

How do you respond to that? I didn't. I walked to the end of the block and met Bunny on the corner.

"Did you get it?"

Bunny handed me the camera with the photos on it. I'd ran into Bunny Goodstuff a few months earlier in Tompkins Square Park. She approached me wondering if I was looking for heroin. I wasn't. She asked if I had any friends looking for heroin. I didn't. She looked desperate, so I offered her fifty bucks if she could put a mic near the two guys I was spying on. She did. Since then I've hired her when I needed someone to get pictures undetected. She was only four-foot-tall so it was easy for her to blend in. I was short on cash after being fleeced by Candi, so I arranged to pay Bunny the following night at the park.

The alarm went off and it felt like I'd only been sleeping for a couple of minutes. I was nervous Dorothy would come up with another excuse to get out of paying me, so I planned on getting to her house early enough to snap pictures of her and her new lover for insurance.

I arrived at her place a little before eight and set up a station in Dorothy's rose bush. I thought about Candi. Even if my love was unrequited, with the money Dorothy was about to pay me I could spend the entire weekend with her. The bald slime bag finally left the house wearing a poorly tailored suit and a purple skinny scarf. As soon as he pulled out of the driveway her new lover came running out of nowhere, letting himself in. She should have installed revolving doors. I ran up to a window and took pictures of them having sex on the floor. The sex was a little too sensual and at times felt a little sluggish. I sat back in my car and waited for him to leave.

Dorothy was delighted with the new evidence, but I could tell she was judging me by the way she was grinding her teeth. She handed me a brown envelope with the six grand she owed me.

"Pleasure doing business with you." I said, quoting Candi.

As I was putting my coat back on Dorothy started flicking through the pictures of Candi and her slime bag husband.

"Who is she?" She asked, pointing to Candi.
"I never caught her name."
"I bet she's a hooker." She said. "The tramp."

I had to bite my tongue.

I let myself out, both fists clenched ready to gouge her two eyeballs out. I wondered if her husband wasn't such a bad guy after all, maybe it was all her. I went through the pictures of her having sex on the floor and decided I'd sell them to the bald slime ball with the skinny scarf. I knew she wouldn't hesitate to call him out on his excursions and he'd be more than willing to spend a few grand on the pictures. I added the 10 pm AA meeting to my calendar and drove back to Manhattan. While driving, my cop friend called me.

They'd found two bodies on Randall's Island, only a few miles from where Quincy Quinn and Susie Jones were last seen. One male, one female, both in their early twenties. A *House of Gains* sports bra in the dead guy's hand and the short shorts around the dead girl's ankles suggested it was them. He said both heads were taken, an ode to Tommy Fogarty.

Candi walked out of her building wearing a tight red dress with matching heels. We made eye contact as she walked by my car, but she didn't acknowledge me. I got out of the car and followed her.

"Candi!"

She stopped and turned around before taking her sunglasses off.

"Do I know you?" She asked.
"Yeah you do." I said. "We had sex last week."
"I've never seen you before in my life."

She turned around and started walking north on Orchard and I followed her.

"We had pancakes."
"Do I look like I eat pancakes?"
"You walked out on the tab."
"I'll pay you back." She said. "Not now though."
"Where are you going?"
"Mind your own fucking business, Mitten." She said.

At least she remembered me.

"I'll give you another two grand for an hour."

She stopped walking.

"Two grand?"
"Two grand."

Ronnie the doorman was awake this time and operated the elevator.

"Have a nice afternoon girls." He said.

Candi never looked at him and grabbed my arm before I could respond. The shower was running but she insisted no one was home. She threw me over her bed and pulled my underwear down from under my skirt. She pulled my legs apart and started going down on me. After orgasming I offered to repay the favor, but she insisted that she didn't have the time. She stuffed the two thousand dollars in her purse while I was putting on my shoes.

"Can I see you tonight?"
"What the fuck is wrong with you?" She asked.

"I like you."
"If you're lonely go get a dog or a boyfriend."

Candi sat on the bed beside me. I could tell she felt sorry for me. She explained she had a full day ahead of her, but said there might be a chance she could fit me in later in the night. I knew she wouldn't.

"I'll call you if I'm free." She said.
"You don't have my number."
"Well, give it to me then." She said. "And stop following me Mitten, it's creepy."

I handed her my business card.

"You're a PI?"
"Do you have some kind of issue with that?"
"I could tell you were some kind of rat." She said. "Let's go."

While we were waiting for Ronnie the doorman we started making out in the hallway. She had the tip of her finger inside me when the elevator doors sprung open.

"Hello ladies."
"Fuck off Ron." Candi said, before whispering in my ear. "I'll see you tonight."
"I'm broke."
"I can make an exception."

I wondered what Ronnie thought we were talking about.

Sitting in my parked car on the crowded street I watched Candi and my two thousand dollars walk away in the side mirror. My phone rang again, this time it was Quincy's mom. The most agonizing part of the conversation was her positive energy. She hadn't learned of the discovery of the two headless bodies and I had no intention of being the one to break the news to her.

"I think we're going to find Quincy today." She said, beaming with excitement.
"I hope so." I said. "I'll call you later."

I had time to kill so I decided to get Phil something to cheer him up. He worked the day shift at a bar nearby. His girlfriend kicked him out a few months earlier sending him further off the deep end, not that Mom had left any shallow water for either of us.

I went to H&M and bought him two new shirts and six pairs of socks. I stopped by his favorite music store and bought a new pair of strings for his busted guitar. I wanted to give him cash too, but knew how he'd spend it. I stopped into Victoria's Secret and picked up something cute for Candi, just in case she called. Scarlet red panties and a matching bra to go with her tight red dress.

Derailed by Candi's lingerie shopping, it was 5:30 pm before I made it to *Patrick's Irish Pub*. An older guy was bartending with his chest stuck out and polo collar popped. I could tell it was Dave.

Phil and Jimmie had told me all about him. Rumor had it he hadn't been capable of sustaining a lasting erection for the better part of a decade and took his sexual frustration out on the staff. He was on the phone.

"He came in wasted and attacked a customer." He said. "He pissed all over my fucking door."

Perhaps the deep end was an understatement.

"Call me if you see him." He said and hung up the phone
as I took a seat at the bar.
"What can I get you?"

I ordered my usual Tanqueray and tonic with two limes
and a lemon. He didn't have Tanqueray so I had to settle
for Sapphire.

"Is Phil not working today?"
"He doesn't work here anymore." He said bullishly.
"Since when?"

Dave gave me a more detailed account of what I'd
overheard and added that Phil stole four hundred dollars
from the register.

"That explains the smell." I said. "Perhaps you're
overreacting?"

Dave wasn't amused and assured me that the cops were
on their way to take a report.

"How do you know that lowlife waster?" He asked.
"That's kind of a long story." I said.

I took four hundred dollars from Dorothy's envelope and
threw it on the bar.

"Here's your money. Tell the cops you made a mistake."
"Not a chance." He said.
"Well then, I guess I'll just come back here tomorrow
and tell all your staff about the time we hooked up."
"What are you talking about?"

"I'll tell them about how you spent the night crying on the floor because you couldn't get hard."

I left the four hundred dollars and a pair of socks next to my empty glass. The most expensive gin and tonic in New York City. After leaving I tried to call Phil, but he let it ring out again. It was a long shot to think he would have gone home after getting fired and pissing all over the bar, but I decided to try his apartment in Bed Stuy.

I got to his place sometime after six letting myself in with the keys he'd given me. His unfurnished apartment was in disarray. The dirty mattress smelled of piss, the floor was covered in beer bottles, empty cocaine bags and some women's underwear. I was standing in a pool of vomit before noticing the handwritten suicide letter.

Mitten, I'm sorry for everyone I caused you.

A typo? Out of the corner of my eye I saw a rat running across the room. The picture he used to have hanging up of Mom was gone, out the window was my guess.

When Mom was healthy, she worked at a diner. We spent most of our childhood sitting at the counter. It wasn't ideal but at least we were never hungry. Once she started using again, we were sent to our aunts who was an evil conservative Christian witch. Phil would always defend Mom saying her sickness was temporary. He kept excusing her into his twenties, until they found her belongings on the side of the Triboro Bridge. Mom was gone.

Her belongings consisted of a flip phone, her engagement ring and two letters addressed to Phil and I. A week later they found her body washed up somewhere in Jersey and Phil still hasn't forgiven himself. I can only speak for myself, but her suicide letter wasn't any more elaborate than Phil's typo filled attempt.

Sorry Mitten, take care of Sweet Phillip.

I put Phil's manifesto in my pocket and let myself out before one of his pets attacked me. I called him again, this time leaving a voicemail.

"Phil, where the fuck are you?"

As much as it pained me to do so, I decided to stop by Jimmie's bar to see if Phil was there.

My ex Jimmie ran *The Pine Box* on St. Marks Place. Jimmie had got Phil the job at *Patrick's Irish Pub* so I knew he was going to be infuriated if he heard about how Phil pissed all over it. Jimmie hated me, but not nearly as much as I hated him.

When I got to the bar the first thing Jimmie did was point to the kitchen demanding that I follow him. Here we go, I thought to myself.

"Have you seen Phil?" I asked.
"Yeah, I've fucking seen him and there's two pigs at the bar looking for him."
"Why?"
"He was in here with some babog a while ago and she slashed the face off some young wan."
"Jimmie, speak English."
"Phil's fucking dead to me." He said.
"He might be."

I showed Jimmie the suicide letter.

"He was never much of an artist." He joked.

"Jimmie!"

"He's always saying he's going to top himself for fuck's sake."

"This is different."

Jimmie told me to wait in the kitchen while he checked on the bar. I couldn't help but recall that this was the last place we had sex. I thought about Candi, trying to distract myself. Jimmie returned complaining about some cunts not leaving a tip.

"Where have you been looking?" He asked.

"He wasn't at Patrick's." I said.

"The dopey prick got fired."

"He wasn't at his apartment either."

"He got evicted."

"So, what should I do?" I asked. "I've been looking everywhere."

Jimmie paused and looked around the kitchen, then at me.

"I swear to God if you try and kiss me right now, I'm going to punch you in the face." I said.

"Try Fred at the desk." He said.

"Who's Fred at the desk?"

Fred worked at the reception of the hotel next door where I had caught the bald slime ball and Candi. He was a well-known personality around the East Village. There was a sign in the lobby that read.

Thirty dollars an hour or one hundred for the night.

That explained why Candi liked the place so much. Fred was obese and spoke with a very feminine voice.

"I'm looking for my brother."
"And I can tell you have a very caliginous soul." He said.
"He's five foot ten, skinny with long hair." I informed him.
"I don't know what I've seen but have you seen me?" He asked. "I'm in a movie, it's called Evil Desires."

This is useless.

"It isn't a porno, but I do get naked a couple of times."

By now it was close to nine pm and I still had to pay Bunny Goodstuff.

"Here's my card." I said. "Can you call me if you see him?"
"They had a stand in for my penis because they said it was too big and gross."

I left.

Tompkins Square Park was one of my favorite places to hang out. I liked my parks how I liked people, seedy with a splash of danger. I would often sit there and reminisce about my life. I sat on a bench near Avenue A where I'd originally ran into Bunny Goodstuff and waited.

I tried to leave Phil another voicemail but some homeless guy in an *I Love the Bronx* t-shirt started blasting Biggie Smalls from a boombox.

Bunny showed up ten minutes later looking like she'd been partying all day. She was barefoot and dressed in a blue pillowcase. She walked by me without saying anything so I had to yell at her.

"Bunny!"

I knew better than to hang out with Bunny while she was drinking so I kept the conversation to a minimum.

"Here's your money." I said handing her the envelope.
"Well it's about fucking time Mitten." She said slurring each word.
"Well it was good to see you too Bunny."

As I was about to get up and leave, she asked if I could return at midnight, insisting she had something important to share with me. I wasn't coming back to the fucking park at midnight, but I went along with it.

"There's a bench on the northeast side by the entrance, next to the white garbage can." She said. "You know the one I'm talking about?"

We were sitting on it.

"Yeah, I know it."
"Meet me there?"
"Sure, I'll see you then."

On my way out, she yelled across the park.

"Cover up your fucking tits Mitten, people are looking at you!"

After leaving the park I text Dorothy's husband and asked if he was going to the meeting. He replied instantly.

I'm on my way babe. ;)

I arrived at the 10 pm meeting a few minutes early, hoping to sell the bald creep the pictures. He wasn't there yet. The speaker shared about how difficult his life was growing up in Nebraska and his new-found love for cream soda.

"Life is short and you have to live everyday like it's your last, because one day you'll be right." He said with his therapeutic Mid-Western innocence.

After his qualification they took a break to pass the basket, two dollars was the recommended donation. A far cry from the four hundred I'd spent on a gin and tonic or the four grand I'd blown on sex.

There was still no sign of the creep. I checked my phone and saw I had two missed calls from Quincy's mom and two texts from my friend the cop.

Two more dead bodies found in Forest Hills, both women.

What were their names?

He didn't respond.

Shortly after the meeting resumed the bald slime bag with the skinny scarf entered. He placed his hand on my leg and apologized for being late. All I could think about was the vile vision of him putting his immoral hands on

Candi's hot naked body. It was too much for me to take and I abandoned the idea of selling the pictures of Dorothy. The Mid-Western speaker called on him to share.

He quoted a random prayer word for word and followed that up with his usual grateful to be alive routine. Once his presentation concluded I decided it was time to go.

"I'll be right back." I smiled at him and whispered.

I took the envelope with the pictures and walked out the door. I could tell he was annoyed with my premature departure but, I needed to talk to Jimmie.

When I got back to the bar Jimmie didn't have a single customer left. He was standing behind the bar flicking through the sports channels.

"Did you find him?" He asked.
"No. I was hoping you did."
"You want a drink?"

I had another gin and tonic and Jimmie poured me shots.

Aside from being an unfaithful piece of shit he was fun to hang out with. I told him about Dorothy and the creep, leaving out the part about Candi. I did four more shots of whiskey in ten minutes and foolishly wound up naked in the women's restroom with him. He turned me around and blew his load all over my chest. Jimmie's signature move. Candi was right, I should have adopted a dog.

"I fucking hate you." I said pulling my underwear back up.

"That's a little harsh Mitten." He said as I washed myself off in the sink.

After getting dressed I sat in the corner and finished my drink. Jimmie made a poor attempt at an apology. He then shared information he should have shared much sooner.

"Phil's babog should have never slashed my customer!"
"Phil's what?"
"He was with a little midget in a blue pillowcase."
"Why didn't you fucking tell me that?"
"I did."
"You didn't."
"I said he was in with a babog."

Bunny was the last person to see Phil alive and could have known where he might be.

"What time is it? I asked.
"Ten to."
"English Jimmie!"
"Eleven fifty."
"I've got to go."
"Okay, it's thirty-two dollars." He said.
"I'll pay you whenever, not now though."

I ran to Tompkins Square Park.

I sat at the northeast corner where Goodstuff asked me to meet her. I ripped up the envelope with the pictures of Dorothy and her new lover and threw them in the garbage can. The homeless man with the boombox was gone and I could actually hear myself think. I thought about the third time I met Jimmie. It was Christmas Day on a nicer park bench in a nicer side of town.

There was still nothing from Phil, but my friend the cop finally text me back.

Sorry for the delay.
Their names were Dorothy and Candi.

Why would Candi be at Dorothy's?

That's why Candi hadn't text me, she was dead. I look up at the night sky, tainted from the city's sea of lights. One clear star shines down so I talk up to it.

If you can hear me, I need help.

5.

Bunny Goodstuff

I woke up on top of a soggy pillow in an unfamiliar gloomy hallway. My cell phone, drugs, money and two guns were all gone. It seemed from the rancid taste in my mouth that I'd been smoking crack and sucking cock. My clothes were nowhere to be found.

There were four closed doors on the floor, but it was unclear which one I may or may not have been inside. I thumped and kicked on all four of them, but I was greeted with the same stillness from each one. I took the pillowcase off the pillow I'd been sleeping on and ripped it into a new dress. I walked out the front door and into mayhem.

Multiple cars and buildings were burning and people were rioting in the streets. Some of the children were holding signs that read:

Build the wall!

There were several baby pigs running down the avenue, being chased by angry young men. That's when it hit me, I was on Staten fucking Island.

Thirty-four years in New York, I'd avoided this putrid place like the plague and here I was stranded on the inbred, disease ridden Island. That's it, I told myself, I'm done smoking crack.

Two men approached me carrying clucking chickens in each hand.

"How the fuck do I get off this island?" I asked them.
"You need a boat."
"No shit!" I yelled. "What boat?"
"The ferry is free." The brains of the operation explained pointing to the docks.

I could see the New York City skyline in the distance across the water. There was a turned over green tricycle lying in a ditch. I jumped on it and rode through the crowds straight to the dock.

"Watch where you're going kid!" An old bitch yelled.
"I'm thirty-four you cunt!"

I hadn't grown since I was seven. Stuck at four foot one for all eternity. When I was young, a doctor once told me I stopped growing because of all the bath salts I was smoking.

I abandoned my tricycle at the docks and boarded the ferry like the hick promised.

Two different types of people use the Staten Island Ferry, dickhead tourists and inbred scumbags. There didn't seem to be any shortage of either of them. I eventually found a seat and sat down trying to piece together how the fuck I ended up on Staten Island.

I remembered doing a quick job with Mitten and then going back to the park. Cracked out George sold me a bunch of crack, but I couldn't remember if I smoked it.

Maybe he knows what happened.

I noticed a dirty Guido drinking a bottle of Heineken.

"Are you going to finish that brother?" I asked, while simultaneously taking it from him.
"That was the plan." He said in fear.

I found a dark corner where I could drink my beer and reflect further on the night before. I didn't want to know what time it was. The sun was up so I knew I was late. I had to be at Chef's every morning at 9 am or he'd slap me. Tommy had been threatening to fire and shoot me for a while now, maybe this was the day he'd actually do it.

I'd met him a year earlier at a homeless shelter I'd been staying at. He would show up every week with food. I'd later find out what he had been putting in it. Tommy put the Good in Bunny Goodstuff and without him I'd be back in line at the food bank, and he liked to remind me of that.

On the way to Manhattan we sailed past the Statue of Liberty. It was the first time I'd ever seen the statue that close. I stood tall and stuck my middle fingers up at her howling.

"Fuck you, you filthy whore!"

That's when I noticed some tourist trying to take a picture of me. He had a fanny pack on around his South Dakota hoodie and binoculars hanging off his fat neck.

"What the fuck are you doing?"
"I was taking a picture." He said.

I snatched the camera out of his sweaty hands and tossed it in the river. He stared at me blank and dumb with his mouth agape.

"Welcome to New York asshole." I said, adding "Don't take pictures of strangers."
"I was taking a picture of the Statue." He said.

His wife who had been trying to console him shouldn't have involved herself.

"You owe us seven hundred dollars for that camera."
"No, you owe me a new beer."

I cracked the top of my Heineken bottle off the floor and used it to cut her leg. She fell to the ground using her two hands to try and conceal the blood. I've always received instant gratification when assaulting women in front of their man. There's so much joy associated with proving to a woman what a dirty pussy her man is.

"Stop!" He yelled, making little effort to hide the tears from running down his red bloated face.
"Someone call the cops." His wife screeched.

"We're on the Staten Island Ferry asshole, you think there are fucking cops?" I reminded them.

After throwing the rest of the bottle at him I warned them both not to follow me. I walked to the other end of the ferry and found a new corner to sleep in. Tommy was making a grand a day from my sales, maybe he would be understanding. The boat docked and my denial started to wear off. I was fucking dead and I knew it. Either I blamed the loss on someone else or Tommy would feed me to every homeless cunt in New York. It was time to face the music and I hailed a cab to the Bronx.

"Gun Hill Road."
"Rough night?" The taxi driver asked.

I laid across the back seat and took a nap. When I woke up, we were going over the Triboro Bridge.

"What time is it brother?"
"Noon."
"What day is it?"
"The thirteenth."
"No, what day of the week is it?

It was Wednesday, our busiest day of the week. By now the meter was up to fifty bucks and I didn't have a dollar on me. Luckily, I hadn't paid for a cab in years. When it comes to scoring a free cab ride, the methods are infinite. The easiest way is to video him on his phone and then blackmailing him. Problem was, I didn't have any electronics. Sometimes I'd open the windows and scream bomb or yell at him for short braking. I was feeling poorly so I went with the safest option and chewed off the seat belts. This took about ten minutes.

Once we were closer to Chef's apartment, I made my accusation.

"You realize you don't have any protection back here right?"
"What are you talking about?"
"The seat belts are both fucked so I'm not paying."
"You pay me right now or I'll call the police."
"Call them then you dirty pussy!" I screamed, shaking my fist.

When I got out of the taxi the driver attempted to follow me. There was a hubcap lying in the gutter that I threatened to smash across his face.

"Yell pay me one more fucking time!" I yelled.

He did.

I threw the hubcap like a frisbee and it landed square on his nose causing a significant amount of blood to gush from his face. When he fell to the ground, he dropped his phone. He had 911 dialed when I dropped it down the drain.

"You dirty fucking pussy." I said emasculating him.

I'd miscalculated how many blocks we were from Chefs so I drove the taxi the rest of the way there. I'd made it about four blocks before crashing into a parked PT Cruiser.

"They parked too far from the curb!" I said to a stranger, before walking the rest of the way up the hill.

Another door unanswered, was anyone home today?
Chef boasted that he was once number four on
America's most wanted list, and as a result he rarely left
the house. I sat and waited on his stoop for the next hour
before deciding to take a walk.

My Grandmother was buried half a mile away from
Chefs at the Woodlawn Cemetery. Like me, Nanny
suffered from a dreadful fear of rats. When she was in
hospice, I had to promise I'd surround her grave with rat
poison. Her biggest fear was that rats would eat her
corpse. She couldn't stand the dread of her decaying
body being in a rat's mouth, chewing on her with its
sharp teeth and then the terror of being in its stomach,
God forbid the vermin defecating her.

Her twin sister died when she was only a few months old
after having her face, fingers and toes consumed by a
treacherous rat. Nanny was in the crib beside her and had
been ridden with survivor's guilt until her death. At the
time of her passing she didn't have a dime left in the
bank. My finances weren't in order either so the church
paid to put her in a fifty-dollar cardboard coffin. The
cardboard wouldn't keep the insects out, let alone the
rats. One day I left my cat Ralph there to protect her, but
either he ran away or the rats got him too.

I always spoke to Nanny loud and clear. I don't believe
that after death dead people can read your fucking mind
like they're all of a sudden clairvoyant. She had poor
hearing when she was alive. After having a chat with
Nanny and explaining how I was going to eventually
steal the money from Chef's safe I walked back to
Tommy's.

I rang the doorbell. This time he was home.

"Hold on!" He screamed so I rang it again.
"Can you give me a fucking second?"

Five minutes had passed before I rang the bell for a third time. He opened the door.

"What part of hold on don't you understand?"
"Hi Chef."

Tommy was naked and had blood all over his hands and genitals.

"What are you up to?"
"I was fucking cooking." He said, adding. "You're late!"
"I was here earlier Chef, you weren't home."
"What time?"
"A little before nine I'd say."

He slapped me across the face with his burger flipper.

"What time?"
"Ten."

He hit me again, this time busting my lip.

"What time?!"
"Okay, twelve."
"You're fucking late!"
"I am."
"What the fuck are you wearing?"
"My new dress."

He threw me inside before slamming the door.

"How much do you have and what do you need?"
"I have nothing and I need the usual."

He slapped me for the third time.

"What the fuck do you mean you've got nothing?
"They robbed me." I said.
"Who fucking robbed you?"

Mitten was the first name that came to mind. If I didn't blame someone Chef would have killed me right then and there.

"Who the fuck is Mitten?"
"Tits that talk." I responded.

I'd ran into Mitten a couple of months earlier at the park. She had no personality, just talking tits. I asked if she was looking for drugs and got offered a job instead. She was a private detective and hired me to be her assistant. She paid well, but was annoying with her nihilistic attitude. I told Chef that after I'd trusted her to help me with a deal, she slipped something in my drink, stealing the drugs, money and two guns.

"She has the fucking guns?"
"Yeah."
"And how much money?'
"Two grand I'd say."
"You fucking cunt Bunny!"

He slapped me in the face and kicked me a couple of times. While I was trying to get off the ground, he pulled out his iPad.

"What's her full name?"
"Mitten Sharpe."
"Are you trying to be funny?"
"That's her name."

He showed me his iPad with a picture of her on it.

"Is that her?"
"It is."

Chef sat down and went through her pictures.

"She has beautiful eyes." He said.
"I guess."
"Her nose is so vulnerable and delicate."
"I suppose."

He started playing with his nipples and making strange sex sounds before jerking himself off beside me.

"I'm going to wash my hands." I said.

He didn't respond.

On my way to the restroom I noticed a fresh human foot lying on his staircase. The toe nails were long and painted black. I followed the blood trail upstairs into Chefs bedroom. The rest of the body was lying across his bed. The head, her foot and part of the stomach had been removed. Some fat from her ass cheeks had also been taken. Tommy loved to collect heads.

The girl's jean shorts and underwear were on the ground next to the bed. The knickers were too big for me, but I put the jean shorts on underneath my pillowcase. I often wondered what corpse tits felt like so I squeezed her breasts. They were mostly the same except cold and a little hard. I could tell she hadn't been dead long. Twenty minutes, maybe less I reckoned. This explained why Chef waited so long to open the door.

When I went back downstairs, Chef was in the kitchen with his dick in one hand and the dead girl's head in the other. He was masturbating to a selfie Mitten had posted on Facebook.

"So, can I get some drugs Chef?" I said interrupting him.
"Can you give me a fucking second?!"

Chef would give me a giant bag of the good stuff every morning that I'd sell for two grand. The next morning I'd bring him a thousand dollars and we'd repeat. I was sitting on the couch when I heard him ejaculate. He screamed yes, a bunch of times. He was a lot more pleasant when he returned to the living room.

"Are you hungry Bunny?"
"No."

Chef didn't take no for an answer and I didn't have to ask to know what was on the menu.

Flesh empanadas with rice and beans.

After years of experience, he had mastered the art of cooking human flesh. Being forced to eat that woman was bad enough, but the fact that her head was on the table staring at me was devastating.

"Could we perhaps close her eyes chef?"
"The eyes stay open." He said.

He put a baker's dozen and his gun on the table encouraging me not to be shy.

"Eat up Bunny."

I took a bite of one of his empanadas and he didn't stop staring at me until I swallowed it all. He smiled and continued eating his own food. The empanadas weren't bad, a little burnt but not bad.

"How's the meat cooked?" He asked.
"Perfect." I said. "Very moist."
"She was very athletic." He said. "You can tell she trained because of how tender the meat is."
"You can, you're right Chef."
"The tramp stayed in shape by having sex with other men."

At that moment it felt very real to me. We ate another empanada each before resuming our conversation.

 "So, tell me more about Mitten."
"Tits that talk." I said. "No personality."
"Is there much fat on her buttocks?"
"A decent amount."

He was satisfied with my description nodding his head as he continued.

"How are you enjoying your lunch?"
"Great, I love it."

Chef was excited by my enthusiasm and wrote out the recipe.

"You don't want to undercook the protein." He said handing it to me. "If you have it rare you could get kuru or salmonella."
"Thanks for the tip."
"Let's take her tonight then." He said, changing the subject.

"If you let me borrow a gun, I'll shoot her myself." I said.

He banged his fist on the table.

"I forgot the wine!" He yelled walking to the kitchen.

Chef was an expert sommelier and suggested a great red wine to go with the empanadas. I'm no wine drinker, but it was nice to wash the girl's ass fat out of my mouth. He sniffed his wine for twenty seconds before saying.

"You won't be killing anyone."
"I won't?"
"I'm going to claim Mitten."
"Whatever you want."
"I'm going to take her head, the meat from her buttocks and her belly fat." He said with contempt.
"That sounds great Chef."

We arranged to meet at Tompkins Square Park at midnight. Every New Yorker knew not to enter Tompkins Square Park that late, even the cops would obey this logic. My job was to lure Mitten there and Chef would take care of the rest.

"Bring her to the southeast corner of the park." He pushed.

I'd already arranged to meet Mitten at nine so having her return a few hours later would be easy. Chef asked me to bring a rucksack for the head and fat. Trying to take her entire body was an unrealistic goal and he insisted that we be pragmatic.

"Well, if you'll excuse me, I have some work to attend to upstairs." He said, picking up a saw.
"Can I get the drugs?"

Still excited with the prospect of butchering Mitten he opened the safe right in front of me. He would normally have me turn around first.

10R-8L-83R

Finally, I had the code. He opened the safe and money fell out on the floor. There must have been a hundred grand in there, easy. He handed me the usual bag of heroin warning me to be more careful and to let myself out. He picked up his saw and walked back upstairs.

Chef had broken out of prison a few years earlier and was presumed dead by the law. Regardless of his phantomlike ending he had to be cautious when going out. After rumors began circulating about numerous sightings and more girls disappearing each week, he had to start wearing a disguise when he left his apartment. Today would be no exception. Traffic was a disaster and it was almost evening before I arrived in the East Village. Once we drove by 14th Street I opened the windows and started making accusations.

"He has a bomb!"

Another free ride.

I stopped off at a Duane Reade on my way to the park and stole a box of one hundred small bags to put the heroin in. After, I went to a coffee shop around the corner and divided the drugs up in the bathroom. The dead girl's jean short pockets were large and I was able to fit twenty bags of heroin in them. I hid the rest inside the toilet tank. After arriving at Tompkins Square Park, the first thing I saw was some sad sap holding a bottle of gin trying to score coke from two undercover cops. They were both black, shirtless and blasting Biggie Smalls from an antique boombox. After getting into a physical altercation with one of the cops the junkie staggered around the park. I followed him for a while.

"What are you looking for?" I asked.
"Drugs, a lot of drugs and I want the good stuff, none of that fucking baking soda."
"I only sell the good stuff." I said introducing myself.
"I want a hundred dollars' worth of cocaine."

The dirty pussy.

"What's your name?" I asked.
"Phil."
"Phil, you're a dirty fucking pussy." I said walking away.
"Where the fuck are you going?"
"I only sell heroin." I told him.

He said that he was scared of needles and hadn't done heroin before.

"Just sniff it then, you dirty pussy."

I needed money fast so I gave him a discount and sold four bags for the price of three. During the transaction I noticed he had a large wad of cash and vowed to come back for the rest. I took a few swigs from his bottle of gin and circled the park. Over the next hour I sold another ten-dollar bag of junk and blew an old guy for fifty bucks in the public restroom. Technically forty, but he tipped me ten. My takings for the day was now at $90 which was decent, but if I had anything less than a grand for Tommy, I'd be getting a lot more than a busted lip. I did another lap of the park and ran into Phil again, who by now was as high as a fucking kite.

"Where are you going?" I asked.

He was slurring his words and drooling like a child, explaining that he had a friend that worked at a nearby sports bar. The alleged friend let him drink for free. Drinking for free seemed like a fun way to spend an hour, before I robbed him blind.

"I'll come too." I said.

His friend worked at *The Pine Box,* a hipster pretentious spot on St. Marks. We finished his bottle of gin on the walk there. When we got to the bar his apparent friend was the furthest thing from friendly, blind with rage.

"You dopey prick!" He yelled at Phil.

Phil apologized on his behalf before following him to the kitchen. I sat at the bar getting antsy waiting for someone to serve me a drink. While minding my own business the cunt next to me had the audacity to touch my arm. Before I had a chance to respond the dirty pussy went on to make disparaging remarks about my outfit.

"Is that a pillowcase?" She asked, laughing in my face.
"Have you ever played with a dead girl's tits?" I asked her.
"Have I ever what?"

I grabbed her wine glass and cracked it off the counter breaking it almost in half. I used what was left of it to stab her in the face. The glass sliced nicely through her perfect skin. The red wine dripped to the floor mixing with blood, forming a puddle between her feet. I took an ashtray from the bar and started smashing it across her once pretty little head. I heard and felt the bones breaking in her face and could tell she regretted the hurtful things she said to me.

Phil and his so-called friend, the bartender, eventually pulled me off her. Their teamwork wouldn't last long and they started arguing again. While they were in the midst of their disagreement, I picked up a piece of glass and used it to cut most of the girl's top lip off. The bartender grabbed me once more, this time inappropriately touching my pussy with his thumb.

"Get your hands off my pussy you fucking cunt!"

They picked me up and stuffed me inside Phil's sports bag like a dog and zipped it shut.

"Motherfuckers!"

In the sweaty darkness I could hear sirens and people yelling while being transported down the busy street. It felt like a hundred and twenty degrees in the bag and I must have yelled at him to let me out fifty fucking times. Finally, he did. We were back in Tompkins Square Park before he unzipped it.

We sat in silence for a half an hour before Phil worked up the courage and apologized for putting me in the bag. He said I'd have been arrested and detained if he hadn't put me in the bag.

"Stop trying to justify your bullshit." I said.
He spent the next ten minutes ranting about Jimmie, his former friend.

"He's a fucking cunt." He said.
"She was a fucking cunt too."
"Not to mention he's married with a kid."
"The homewrecking whore." We laughed.

Phil snorted a line of the good stuff and passed out with some drool running down the side of his mouth. I pulled out his wallet and stole three hundred dollars out of it, leaving him a twenty- and seven-dollar bills so he wouldn't notice it was gone. While stuffing his money in the dead girl's jean shorts, he woke back up.

"You see that star?" He said pointing to the now black sky. "What should we call it?"
"Savage." I said.

It was still roasting in the park and I took off my pillowcase to cool down. Phil who was still a bit dazed from the heroin started sucking on my tits.

"Whoa!" I said. "If you want to fuck you have to pay me first."
"How much?" He asked.

I couldn't risk him going through his wallet and finding out that he had been robbed so I said he could fuck me for free this one time, as long as he didn't blow his load inside me. I took off the dead girl's jean shorts and he pressed me against a tree fucking me from behind.
Unlike Tommy, Phil had no issue ejaculating.

"What the fuck Phil?" I said. "You were supposed to pull out."
"I'm sorry Bunny."

I told him that he had to give me money for a pill to kill the unwanted baby.

"How much?" He asked.
"Twenty-seven dollars."

After he paid me, Phil and I laid back in the grass and he passed back out. My tally was now up to $417, still well short of two grand I owed Chef. I went back to work and circled the park again. During my second loop I heard someone calling my name.

"Bunny!"
"Mitten!"

I'd totally forgot about Mitten and that we were supposed to be executing her at midnight. She handed me an envelope with two hundred dollars in it for the job we did the night before, driving my gross up to $617.

The talking tits always spoke down to me when we were speaking. After a brief interaction, I invited her back to the park to hang out with Chef later. She agreed to meet me at midnight and like that we were set. Her tits were bursting out of her tight black tank top and I told her to cover them up before she left. She rolled her eyes. I couldn't wait for Chef to cut her head off and to fiddle with her cold dead tits.

Since I'd lost my phone, I had no way of notifying Chef that we were set for midnight, so I walked to a nearby bar and used their pay phone.

131

"We're all set for Midnight brother." I said.
"I'm following her right now." He responded. "Bring a knife for the fat."

I still had some time to kill so I ordered a pint. I didn't stay for long. I had a beer and stole a knife from the kitchen. On my way back to the park I found a small cardboard box for Chef to store the head in. I pulled out the recipe Chef had written on the ripped envelope. His address was on the other side of it.

123 East Gun Hill Road

I thought about that safe in his living room and the prospect of emptying it. He would be so distracted with Mitten's belly fat that he wouldn't notice me robbing him.

I arrived at the southeast corner a little before midnight. There was no sign of either of them yet so I hid in the bushes behind the park bench. By now the park was near empty, with the exception of a few sleeping homeless men. The sound of rats squeaking echoed around the park, which was terrifying. I decided if Mitten showed up first, I'd slice her throat open as an offering to win back Chef's trust. I took my knife out and started sharpening it off the curb.

I spent ten minutes waiting in the bushes but there was no sign of Mitten. As I was about to leave, Chef showed up in full costume and sat on the bench in front of me. When he started peeling off his fake red beard, I could tell something was wrong. I climbed over the fence and sat next to him.

"Hey Chef."

"Where's Mitten?" He asked.
"No sign of her."
"Imagine that."

I suggested that maybe she went to the wrong side of the park and we agreed to go take a look. After taking a couple of steps north I heard a gunshot ring around the park and felt a thump in my back. Tommy started kicking me around on the ground, yelling something about how Mitten and I were in cahoots. He kicked the spot the bullet went through in my back.

"You were in fucking cahoots you little midget bitch."

He stepped on my head and used the muzzle of the gun to burn through my face. He continued yelling some insane shit about how I'd forced Mitten's vulnerability on him. He put the gun to my head and said he'll see me in Hell.

I focus on the lettering of his t-shirt to distract myself from the upcoming execution and pain.

I Love the Bronx.

6.

Ace

A full day had passed and Frown was still stuck to the trap. The bait had no doubt been planted by one of the *Two-Legged Things.*

It seemed *They* would stop at nothing to try and kill *Us*.

"Hang in there." I said in an attempt to inspire her, but her silence felt like an uninspired no.

Suddenly, the door swung open and in burst the *Two-Legged Thing* like a tornado. *It* paid no attention to Frown and collapsed on *Its* nest.

Out of terror, I stayed in the corner of the wall until the light was replaced with darkness. My reentrance was premature as *It* returned while I was on top of *Its* nest.

I froze in shock and looked right at *It*.

By the time the *Two-Legged Thing* had left the room I occupied it was too late, Frown was gone. Dead and discarded I imagined.

I stayed inside until the star in the sky concluded its decline, finally *It* was gone and darkness was once again upon us.

Our time to shine.

"Dusk means busk." Jewel's words echoing through my mind. The sound of my past lovers' voice in secure safer times. This was a memory so distant from reality, so far from me. Time passes, what's done is done and even if she was alive today, she'd be a stranger like the rest. They called her Jewel, but to me she was so much more, so precious.

I no longer obtained an identity, not even a name. Just another criticized creature wandering the soil lost, dejected and alone. Once upon a time someone close to me called me Ace, but everyone was gone.

Some departures were more gruesome than others.

This was not the first time I'd felt the heat on my back, and I too had experienced the burn of the day on the little fur that was left on my disheveled dying frame.

Rat.

The word the *Two-Legged Things* used to describe *Us*. A gross fucking *Rat*.

"They're the ones that are scared of you." Jewel would say before she passed.

She was ravaged and devoured by one of *Us*. When I found Jewel, her heart had been ripped out and it was left by her side.

Rat had a negative connotation to the *Two-Legged Things*, used to describe deceit and betrayal.

It wasn't their ignorance that annoyed me as much as it was the *Rats* who embraced it, *Rats* referring to one another as *Rats*.

Give me mercy.

Turning on one another and feasting on their young. *Rats* aimlessly killing *Rats* for nutrition when there was bread.

What happened to *Us*?

I've never been able to intellectualize it, the violence. A world where supply exceeded the demand, but generosity was weighed down by the greed, the gluttony.

I have always envied the *Two-Legged Things* and their compassion.

Where *They* held empathy, *Rats* held apathy.

Where *They* were united, *Rats* were divided.

Where *They* loved, *Rats* fought to the death.

Some nights I would isolate under the *Two-Legged Things* vehicles where I'd sniff the carbonic acid. The vertigo gave me temporary relief from the mourning, but it proved time and time again to be nothing but a short distraction.

Despite inhaling the fumes I'd cry myself to sleep, blind from the misery. One night I walked in front of a moving vehicle hoping it would take me. It missed or I missed and yet again I spent the night alone.

Suicidal and high on fumes when all I wanted was for something to lift me up and tell me Ace, I wished someone still called me Ace, everything's going to be okay.

Why do I do this to myself? Why the will to exist?

This is no life to live.

The part I struggled with the most was the disgust from the *Two-Legged Things*.

Sometimes *They'd* scream, cross the street or even kick me. All I am to *Them* is just another squeaking *Rat*, a disease-ridden pest. My existence, my basic preservation they had declared an infestation.

After getting into a recent fight with another notch in the gutter, I had this cracking in my chest. It made me squeak louder than I could imagine. This was troublesome for a rat whose self-preservation depended on the ability to remain subtle.

Once the star had vanished from the sky, I made my way to find food. My first obstacle was sound.

A *Two-Legged Thing* was blasting loud vibrations from a device, with it came a force of wind that began blowing in my direction causing me to hunt in unfamiliar territory.

I made my way into a bush trying to figure out my next move.

I wasn't alone.

"You looking at me, *Rat*?" *It* said staring at me with *Its* two demon like eyes.

"I'm no *Rat*." I said, not backing down.

This *Rat* was similar to me in size, but *Its* claws were twice the length. *It* leaped on top of me biting off most of my back leg.

This was a head start I couldn't afford to give anyone in my already fragile state. *It* sunk *Its* sharp claws into my stomach and bit off half my ear. As I tried to run away, *It* leaped on my back and bit off the rest of my ear.

It was never a good day when I could see my own red blood. The sight of my ear dangling from *Its* mouth set me into a blind rage. I managed to somehow throw *It* off my back. In one powerful movement I chewed *Its* throat out, killing *It* instantly.

I laid down and rest my head on *Its* dead back.

"Why couldn't you just leave me be?"

There had to be more to life than this, more to it than killing other *Rats* for survival. My brief serenity was spoiled by a *Two-Legged Thing* screaming.

It mentioned something about how I was disgusting and gross before throwing an enamel object in my direction. Reality was hard to accept sometimes. It was even harder to escape.

Hobbling on my three legs I walked towards the sound of traffic and sneaked underneath a still vehicle. I sniffed the polluted air holding in my breath.

The fumes went straight to my head and for a split moment I forgot about how disgusted I was with the world, for a moment I thought I was going to be okay.

Still bleeding, I staggered and found myself in another isolated bush.

I wasn't alone.

I felt sharp teeth scratching on my back. One of my female peers was sitting by me. She reminded me of Jewel, pretty and sweet with adorable energy. I was grateful she wasn't looking for a fight.

"What are you tired or something?" She asked.
"I got into a fight, it bit off my leg."
"Well good thing you have three more."
"It bit off my ear too."
"Merely an accessory."

She turned around and waited for me to get on top of her. Despite being injured I got on her back and put my cylinder into her chamber penetrating her.

It was my first-time mating since Jewel left forever. It was heaven alright. My lack of a back leg caused me to slip out at the end and I sprayed my sprays all over her tail.

"What's your name?" she asked?
"I don't really have one." I told her. "But once they called me Ace."

Her name was Motto and her eyes were shining under the moonlight. The second time we mated my sprays entered her chamber. After, she asked me if I was hungry and when I said yes, she said to follow her.

We found some bread with a nice texture to nibble on and shared a sugary liquid.

For a second, I felt like we were so much more than the *Rats* that the *Two-Legged Things* branded us to be.

All the bad times, it felt could even just for a second, be outweighed by the good.

I thought to myself that if I'd died right there, I would be thankful for having lived.

I was unaware that I would.

You're going to be okay she said before licking the liquid from my chin. After feeding, I put my cylinder in her chamber for the third time. A perfect ending to the perfect night.

"I have to go now." She said before leaving me.

While trying to find my way back home a *Two-Legged Thing* came close to stepping on me. *It* screamed out the word gross before kicking me into a nearby bush.

The impact had broken the bones in my back and paralyzed me, I was unable to move.

I called out Motto's name but to no avail, just like everyone else I ever loved, Motto was gone.

I laid on the ground, waiting to die.

I had lost perception in my right eye and the left wasn't doing much better. I thought about Motto and that time she licked my face and I'd sprayed my sprays in her chamber.

This caused me to smile.

I was dying and smiling which had long been my wish.

If only *Rats* were capable of photosynthesis.

Then the *Two-Legged Things* would look at us and smile like they do when they look at the plants and the violence would end.

Then I realized I wasn't alone.

This wasn't the kind of company I had so desperately hoped for.

I was surrounded by seven hungry and troublesome *Rats*.

There were no words, only silence, no dialogue was necessary.

They jumped on top of me and began feeding.

I was awake and alive and felt every bite.

My stomach first, then my back and my face.

Thank you, Motto, for showing me love.

I smile.

7.

Jimmie

It was half fucking three and me bleedin' head wrecked and another cunts baby was crying in the other room. A child belonging to some other lanky prick and I'm supposed to be raising the fucking thing.

"Love, that yoke of a thing is crying again" I said to her.

She didn't respond, pretending to be asleep again. That yoke had the whole neighborhood woke and she thought I'd reckon she was sleeping.

"I'll tend to it so, I suppose." I said.

I spent the walk down the hall in the dark wondering at what point my life had started going to shite. Where's a fella like me supposed to even start pondering? Getting kicked out of school and not getting an education wasn't a good start.

I turned on the light in the bedroom and picked up the crying babog that didn't belong to me. There I was, holding another man's child because I convinced myself I could settle down with a bird that was seven weeks pregnant. My bleedin' head wrecked and no longer in love with your one pretending to be asleep in the next room. Sometimes I'd wonder what the fuck I was even doing in New York.

I was born on the shitty side of Dublin in 1983. My father was a pimp who often beat and raped his prostitutes, including my mother, Rose.

In April 1989 he murdered her while I was outside playing Gaelic with some of the lads. He got life in prison, life life, not twenty years or some shite, never seeing the outside world again, actual life life. My aul wans aunt Nora raised me and, in her defense, she did the best she could.

When I was ten, I slapped the head off some lad and got kicked out of school. This was supposed to be a form of punishment but I was delighted. It freed up my afternoons so I could concentrate on what I really wanted to do, watch American TV shows.

Jerry Springer and the Wrestling Federation were my two favorites. I became obsessed with America and their blatant lunacy. I convinced my cousins I'd eventually move over there. They told me there wasn't a fucking chance I'd do anything.

On my eighteenth birthday, a period when I was heavily addicted to shooting heroin, I went up to some cunt standing at the ATM with a needle and robbed him.

"Give me your money or I'll give you fucking AIDS."

A fair and lucrative deal, but you'll always run into a hero eventually, even in Dublin.

I was sentenced to seven years in prison by a judge who died the next day. My plans of moving to America were banjaxed or at least suspended, but my one consolation was at least I'd finally be able to murder my father.

However, the pricks sent me to Mount Joy, nowhere near my scumbag of a father. I spent the first week in jail dope sick and got into a fight with two screws. I spent the next three weeks in solitary confinement with no light. After getting out of there I couldn't score any heroin.

I asked an aul lad called Bobby if he could hook me up with gear and he dragged me to a NA meeting he chaired at the prison. Bobby was serving two life sentences for a double homicide but was grateful to be sober. Sometimes I still wondered why he hadn't killed himself.

I ended up getting sober in August 2001 and counted days at the prison meeting with Bobby and two lads from Stab City, Limerick, Simon and John Paul. JP relapsed a few months later and got life for slicing some poor cunts throat in the middle of the night because he was snoring. The poor bastard was lying in the bed under me at the time. As fucked as it was, we were pretty happy that the snoring stopped.

The hardest part of being sober in prison is the boredom. Second is having to put up with the noise and other cunts being dope sick. Luckily, we had a VCR at the jail and a few local channels on the TV. I watched the towers come down on September 11th and the subsequent coverage of the aftermath.

I became obsessed with New York City.

"I'm moving to New York when I get out of this kip."
I'd tell the lads.
"You'll go fuckin' nowhere." They'd tell me back.

Sometimes the only motivation a person needs in a Dublin prison is a little spite. Some cunt would tell me I couldn't do something or how I couldn't stay clean in jail, so I'd become obsessed with proving them wrong.

Years went by and I saw a lot of people come and go, but August 12th 2007 I was a free man. Nora was brown bread by the time I got out of jail, but she left a few bob in a Credit Union account for me.

The first thing I did was withdraw the money, the second thing I did was book my flight to New York and the third thing I did was get a decent fish n' chips. The last thing I did in Dublin was buy a bottle of holy water, a vase full of lilies and visited Nora's grave for the first and last time.

"I'm sorry I was such a scummy fuck, Nora." I said to her cheap looking headstone that I knew no one else would ever visit.

I pulled the weeds off her grave and placed the lilies on the soil for her. I watched the sun go down behind the trees and thought about some of the things Nora told me over the years. She was the only reason I had the slightest bit of good in me.

"Thanks, Nora." I said. "Thanks, and goodbye."

I flew to New York the following morning.

"How long are you visiting the United States for?" The fat fuck of a border patrol cop asked me.
"A week."
"What's the reason for your visit?"
"Going to watch the Jets."

I thought the Jets were a baseball team so I'm glad he didn't ask any other questions. I was surprised when he stamped my passport but fuck, I thought, New York here I come.

As we flew over New York City I pulled up the little curtain and looked out over my new home, the land of promise, the place where peasants like me came to be kings. I was twenty-four years old and this was the United States of America!

August 13th 2018

Ten years in America and nothing to show for it, but a baby that wasn't mine. The gaff wasn't mine either. My American Dream was dead. I thought about how much I hated Mitten, I'd never loved anyone like the way I loved Mitten, but Jesus Christ I hated her guts. Colette, the mother of the other man's baby called my name.

"Everything okay Jimmie?"

I knew the bitch wasn't asleep.

Mitten text me one afternoon to let me know that she thought I was worthless.

You're worthless, Jimmie!

I text her back saying that I married Colette and I didn't want to see her again. She never text me back.

Sometimes the loudest bang of all is silence. I wasn't married or even engaged, just stuck.

It was 3:33 am and I'd only just got home from work and here I was again, working. I went back to bed and kissed Colette on the forehead and closed my eyes. Just as I was starting to drift off again the baby started crying, this time even louder than before.

Silence is like water, you only miss it when it's taken away. The sound of silence, I spent years of my life dreaming of it. I hated Mitten.

"Christ, that yokes at it again" I said to her.

Colette didn't respond. Asleep with one eye open, no doubt.

Sometimes I felt like a dope complaining. In comparison to the old days I was doing grand. I had fuck all, but it was a lot more than what I used to have. I had a private jax where I could be alone. I had the option of getting a glass of water if I woke up in the middle of the night. I no longer had to listen to old men jerking off, that was huge.

It could have been a lot worse, but I also felt like I could have achieved so much more. I'd taken up acting and a bit of writing when I moved to the States, but it's hard to be a famous actor when you don't have a social security number. Writing was hard.

From the day the towers came down, being an illegal immigrant in America was an ordeal. I couldn't start a bank account, I couldn't get a driver's license and the only work I could get was at dive bars.

Mitten once told me she'd marry me so I could get a Green Card, but I didn't want to give her the satisfaction of doing something nice.

I woke up in bed with a bird named Dawn one morning in the summer of 2011. I walked to the kitchen in my boxers and poured myself a glass of water.

"Who are you?" I heard echoing behind me.

She was perfect, nothing else needs to be added.

"What the fuck are you doing in my kitchen?"
"I'm having a glass of water." I said, adding "I'm hanging out with your roommate."
"Marissa?" She asked.
"That sounds about right." I said.

She left and I went back to the bedroom.

"Don't worry about Mitten, her mother killed herself last year so she's been in a bit of a mood since." Her roommate told me.
"How did she kill herself?"

I'm not sure why that was the first question I asked.

"She jumped off the Triboro Bridge."

I started kissing Dawn's neck and was about to take her shorts back off.

"You're so bleedin' gorgeous, Marissa." I said.

Fucking Mitten.

A year later, sometime in 2012, Mitten wandered into *The Pine Box* where I worked, drunk with her piss head of a brother Phil. He was loaded and quickly fell asleep on the bar counter. I would have kicked them both out but I was trying to place how I knew Mitten.

"Does he want a bleedin' pillow or what?" I asked.
"He'll wake up in a minute." She said. "Give him a minute."
"Where do I know you from?" I asked.
"You don't know me."
"I do and it's wreckin' me bleedin' head."

Phil was asleep for the next three hours. Mitten and I didn't chat much after that. When he woke up, he ordered a Jack and coke. Mitten was tipsy so she didn't try and intervene with Phil's irresponsible bullshit. Who was I to refuse the man a drink? I heard Phil talking about his dead mother and how it was his fault that she died.

"You didn't push her off the bridge." Mitten said.
"Mitten!" I yelled.

She looked at me.

"Remember me?" I asked "I met you in your kitchen last year."

She said she remembered me, but seemed ingenuine. Soon after that, Mitten and Phil got into an argument and she left. This wouldn't be the last time Phil fucked everything up for us. I wouldn't see her again for nearly two years.

When I woke up at eleven Colette and the baby were gone. I didn't have work until seven so I just laid around on the couch. I turned on the TV and watched some talk shows reliving my youth. This was the typical life of an illegal Irish bartender and failed writer living in New York City. Nothing to do until seven pm.

The third time I met Mitten was Christmas Day 2014. The happiest memory from my childhood was when Nora gave me a bike for Christmas. She had been pulling extra shifts at the bookshop where she worked and had been saving up for months. This gesture was something I couldn't even comprehend.

Why would someone put in extra work somewhere they hated just so they could make another person happy?

Nora said my reaction was worth it and that there was nothing she could have purchased for herself that could have replicated that feeling.

Every Christmas Day since moving to New York I would go to the Rockefeller Center Christmas tree and think of Nora. I thought about the future and dreamed of a life that'd be worth living. I turned to my left and my dreams were shaken back to the present.

Have Yourself a Merry Little Christmas was playing
from the speakers and Mitten was sitting right beside me
looking at the same tree. She looked at me and we both
stared back at the tree. I sat in silence wondering if she
remembered me. *Merry Christmas Ya Filthy Animal* was
written across her jumper. She had mittens on.

"You're that guy from the bar, the bartender, right?"
"I was also the guy in your kitchen."

We sat in silence for what felt like an eternity.

"Shouldn't you be with your family?" She asked.
"They're all either dead or in jail." I responded.

We sat in further silence for a moment. I tried to think of
something to say and this was the best I could come up
with.

"How's Dawn?"

Why the fuck would I bring that up?

"I moved out." She said.
"What are you doing here?" I asked.
"I come here every year."
"Me too."
"Well then maybe I'll see you next year." She said
before leaving.
"Maybe."

I watched her walk away, waiting for her to turn around,
waiting for her to say something, but she didn't.

A year of doing the same shite over and over passed by.
I looked at the same blank page for most of it and dated

a couple of people on and off, but most of the year was spent thinking about Mitten and bartending.

Christmas Day 2015, I sat under the tree at Rockefeller Center alone. I sat there for two bleedin' hours staring at the fucking tree. *Have Yourself a Merry Little Christmas* started blasting through the speakers and I looked to my left, then to my right, with no trace of Mitten.

If this had been a Christmas movie she would have been standing under the lights and we would have walked into each other's arms before kissing. It would have been a spectacle, a Christmas miracle, and then we'd walk south east to Grand Central and live happily ever after. There is no such thing as happily ever after, everything has an expiration date, especially love.

The next year was one of the worst years I had in New York. My apartment building burned down and I lost everything, including fifty grand cash I'd kept hidden in the mattress. Almost a decade of bartending in New York City and listening to drunks talking shite for nothing. The saddest part of it was my cat Loki passed away at five years of age, unrelated to the fire. The year couldn't have ended any better though.

The fourth time I met Mitten was Christmas Day 2016. I sat alone under the tree at Rockefeller Center without an ounce of expectation. I thought about Nora and I wished for better things in 2017.

I got up to leave and there she was, standing in front of me like something out of a Christmas movie, staring at me with the same Home Alone sweater on, *Merry Christmas Ya Filthy Animal.*

"You're a year late." I told her.
"Better late than never, right?"

I smiled and she smiled and I'm not sure if either of us
even knew what we were smiling about.

"I meant to say this two years ago, but I love your
jumper."

I walked her back to her Carroll Gardens apartment that
night. We kissed for the first time as we walked over the
Brooklyn Bridge. She looked flawless with the lights of
Lower Manhattan shining on her face. On the walk
home, she told me she was worried about her brother
who had spent the last six months on tour and inebriated.

She moved into my now minimalistic Astoria apartment
that April. The next six months were the best I've ever
had. It was productive, creative, and for the first time in
my life I felt awake. I told Mitten things I hadn't told
anyone and she had some pretty deep stories to share
herself. She urged me to follow my passion for writing,
encouraging me that I had the talent to be doing more
with my life other than withering away behind a bar.

I started writing a book and pushed Mitten to pursue her
photography career. We fought sometimes but the
makeup sex made it worthwhile. We were great for each
other, but like everything in life, this too had an
expiration date and everything would soon turn to shite.

Her brother Phil had spent those months in and out of
rehab, psych wards and on and off our couch. I tried to
be patient but he was wreckin' me bleedin' head. He was
one of the most talented musicians in New York, but to
call him a fucked-up disaster would be polite.

I saw a bit of my younger self in him so I tried to help as much as I could. Bobby put up with me when I first got sober in prison and I tried to share some knowledge from the rooms with him.

Despite trying to twelve step Phil countless times, he still offered me cocaine every time I saw him.

Like Nora, Mitten was a giver not a taker and it felt like she dedicated her entire life to helping her brother. That June of 2017 Phil had put together a few months clean and reached out to me about a job. We weren't hiring at *The Pine Box*, but I put him in touch with Dave from *Patrick's Irish Pub*. A few months after he started working there his girlfriend dumped him and he picked back up.

After the relapse, Phil stole Mittens debit card and took eight hundred dollars from her checking account. Furious, I told her enough was enough and she needed to cut him off. She listened in silence. By the time I got home that night she was gone. I put the book I was writing down and haven't picked it up since.

A week after Mitten left, I ran into Colette. I thought she was the sensible, down to earth girl from Kansas I needed. We'd been hanging out for a month when she told me she was two months preggers.

I was thirty-three and sticking by her felt like the grown-up thing to do. I moved into her loft in Williamsburg and have lived there since. I thought I could deal with the pregnancy thing better than I did, but every month that went by and the bigger she got made it tougher and tougher. In hindsight I should have left then, but for whatever reason I felt this undying loyalty toward her.

The first time I cheated on Colette was Christmas Day 2017. She was six months pregnant at the time with that lanky prick's child. That morning I had promised myself I wasn't going to go to the tree. I'd spent most of the day in the Upper West Side with Colette and her grandparents.

Her grandmother was super conservative so we had to lie and tell them I was the father and the wedding was set before the child was born.

They played jolly Christmas music, had *A Christmas Story* on repeat and I felt fucking nauseous. After the movie started for the third time, I picked up the remote and changed it. At first, I was relieved to have anything else on the television, then *Home Alone* cut to the movie in the movie and that old bastard said it.

"Merry Christmas Ya Filthy Animal."

I lied to Collette and told her I had to chair an AA meeting at 9 pm.

"You never mentioned that."
"I forgot." I said "I'll come pick you up after."

For the first time, when I got to Rockefeller Center, Mitten was there before me. This time I was the one that stood next to her and when she turned her head left, I was the one standing there. This felt like a small victory in of itself.

"How's it going?" I asked.
"Pretty bad, you?"

I was so glad to hear that. The last thing I needed to hear was that she was doing great. I loved her but I couldn't accept it.

"Awful." I told her.

That was the first time I'd been honest to someone in weeks.

"Good, I was worried you were doing well." She said.

She took my hand and held it in silence for the next ten minutes.

"How's the wife?" She asked.
"She's great."
"I can't believe you're going to be a father."

I didn't correct her, instead we started making out.
I put my hand up her sweater and something felt off.

"You got a boob job?"
"Yeah."
"What the fuck did you go and do that for? They were perfect before."
"I'll see you next year." She said before leaving.

As per usual, not so much as a glance back. From that night on I went off the rails and started cheating on Colette sometimes three or four times a week. My record was eight. The baby was born on March 17th, St Patrick's Day.

While Collette was in labor, I was in the jax with some girl called Kristina at *The Pine Box*. Funny enough,

Collette named the baby Kristina, an inside joke that I would never get to tell her.

It was 5 pm, two hours before I had to be at work when I got a phone call from Dave. Phil had assaulted a customer and stole four hundred from the cash register.

"Nice reference shithead." Dave yelled down the phone. "I'll get you the money back man."

One of the most infuriating parts of the breakup was that the dopey prick Phil still came by *The Pine Box* five or six nights a week. The night before, he had come in and drank himself stupid for three hours and then left without saying a word or even attempting to put a bob on the counter. I was ready to slap the head off him.

I left for work at six excited because this bird I'd met the week prior was coming by. Una, a college student with a thing for Irishmen. She was twenty-one and a great way to distract myself from myself.

Una and a few bars of Cadbury's chocolate would get me through to the weekend. I stopped by her NYU dorm and picked her up before she walked me to work. I sat down in the corner and directed the daytime bartender to give her a free glass of wine.

I was no sooner behind the bar when Phil showed up covered in vomit and piss stains.

He was accompanied by a midget wearing nothing but a blue pillowcase. Bunny Goodstuff he called her. She was the spitting image of the bride of Chucky, except way more evil looking. I yelled at Phil to get his ass in the kitchen.

The first thing he said was that he was after being evicted from his gaff and needed a place to crash, like there was any chance I could bring him home to Colette and Kristina. I told him to fuck off and stay with the fifty-year-old stripper he was riding.

Phil handed me forty bucks and apologized for walking out the night before. After I took the cash, we heard a loud crash coming from the bar.

Bunny Goodstuff had cracked an ashtray over Una's head, denting in the side of it. By the time we got out to them she had rearranged her face too. I grabbed Goodstuff and pushed her to the ground.

I turned around and started screaming at Phil. While we were yelling at one another the babog started cutting off Una's top lip with a piece of broken glass. I took the midget by the head and dragged her across the floor. Phil and I put her in the large hockey bag he had been carrying.

"Get your hands off my fucking pussy you cunt!" She yelled at me.

I zipped the bag shut.

I grabbed Phil by the shirt and warned him if I ever saw him again, I'd slap the head off him. After they left, I called Una an ambulance. Una went into a state of shock and sat quietly while the paramedics treated her injuries.

I was a nervous wreck that Collette was about to find out about Una. I spotted Phil two grand the month before he relapsed so he could get an apartment. That was 75% of everything I had and there was no way I could put a deposit down if Colette kicked me out.

While I was outside, I saw the most notorious dirtbag in New York walk by. Bruce Cruz was one of the most full of shite wankers you could ever meet. He was wearing a suit that was way too big for him and a women's skinny scarf, but to his credit he had the best-looking prostitute I'd ever seen with him. She was wearing a red dress with a rose tattoo around her thigh. This was the same scumbag that would be in the rooms singing about how spiritually fit he was.

I saw two detectives standing by the ambulance whom I approached. I told them right off the bat that I had no clue who the babog was and it had fuck all to do with me. The bigger cop had a fucking attitude on him. They asked me if I worked at *The Pine* Box, despite the fact it said *The Pine Box* and the word staff on my black polo.

Against my will they made me give a statement. I've learned over the years that when talking to the filth you have to pick and choose your lies and make sure they balance out. I was honest about my infidelity and couldn't believe how judgmental the cops were.

"There's no law about cheating." I warned them.

I had to take them down to the office and show them the cameras. Watching Bunny Goodstuff cracking the ashtray off Una's head was tough. The cops started judging my decision to put ashtrays on the bar since people weren't allowed to smoke. They were relentless.

I wasn't all that surprised when they recognized Phil, but I didn't expect to be stuck to the wall with a cop screaming in my face.

This was when I started lying, although in hindsight, I should have told them the truth.

"He's just some loser that comes in here now and again." That part was true.

I told them his name was Phil but that was all I knew about him. I mentioned that he was in the night before and didn't pay, which is why I dragged him to the kitchen.

I was surprised they believed me.

While I was mopping Una's blood off the floor, Mitten walked in. It was a little less romantic than our previous encounters. By now, I was fucking furious and couldn't have even pretended to be happy to see her.

The two cops were drinking at the bar so I signaled her to follow me to the kitchen and she did. The last time we were in that kitchen together we had sex. I wondered if she was thinking that as well. She asked me if I'd seen Phil and I filled her in on his latest escapade.

While I was talking shite about him, she showed me a suicide letter she'd found in his bedroom.

I'm sorry for everyone I caused you.

Only Phil could fuck up his one-line suicide letter, the sad matchstick man was a nice touch though.

Mitten was about to start crying so I held her hand and stared into her eyes. For a moment, it felt like we were back at Rockefeller Center on Christmas night.

"I swear to God if you try and kiss me right now, I'm going to punch you in the face." She said.

I told her Phil would probably end up crashing at the hotel slash whore house upstairs. Fred at the desk would come by the bar sometimes, I told her she should go next door and talk to him.

The cops walked out on their check, not a bob down on the fucking bar. Mitten left too.

The rest of the night was dead, from 10 pm on I sat by myself watching ESPN and decided I'd close up at midnight. An hour before I did Mitten came back. She sat down on the same barstool where Una had her head dented in.

"Did you find him?" I asked.
"No. I was hoping you did."
"You want a drink?"

I poured her a Tanqueray and tonic and a shot of whiskey before we said anything.

It was just like the second time we met, except now Phil wasn't asleep on the counter. I could tell she wanted to drink so I poured her a couple more shots before joining her on the other side of the bar.

We started making out at the bar counter and I carried her to the women's jax, by the time I had locked the door she had taken off her underwear. It was hot and I didn't last long. I pulled out of her just in time and came across her new chest.

"I fucking hate you!" She said.
"That's a little harsh, Mitten."

She stormed out of the bathroom into the empty bar.

"What the fuck is your problem?" I asked her.
"You are my fucking problem." She said. "Why don't you ever just go away?"
"I'm working, you came in here."
"Why did you have to leave me?" She asked.

This confused me.

"You left me." I told her.
"I had to leave, you gave me an ultimatum and Phil needed me."
"Fuck you." I said.
"Fuck you." She said.
"Fuck you." I said repeating myself. "I never gave you an ultimatum, I never said, or else."

I couldn't remember if I did or not, but I was relieved when she changed the subject.

"A month after I left you, you shacked up with her."
"What the fuck is shacked up?"
"You have a wife and kid."
"That's some lanky pricks baby." I stated. "If you stop acting like a cunt, I'll leave her and we can be together."
"Well how can I resist an offer like that?"

Mitten was being outrageous, this was all Phil's fucking fault. I changed the subject.

"Phil's babog should have never slashed my customer!"
"Phil's what?"
"He was with a little midget in a blue pillowcase."
"Why didn't you fucking tell me that?"
"I did."
"You didn't."

I told her that he was in here with a babog and then she really flipped.

"What time is it? She asked.
"Ten to."
"English Jimmie!"
"Eleven fifty."
"I've got to go."
"Okay, it's thirty-two dollars." I said.
"I'll pay you whenever, not now though." She said
before leaving, not even a glance back.
"Where are you going now?"

I figured I wouldn't see her again until Christmas Day. I
locked the front door and started the close out sheet. I sat
at table five and started counting the money.

As I finished up, I felt water dripping on my head. That
fucking hotel. The hotel reception was next door but the
actual rooms were right on top of us. Some nights if I
turn the music down, I can hear creeps having sex with
the hookers up there. That bald fucker Bruce Cruz,
would be up there seven nights a week.

I thought about Colette and that baby I promised to treat
like my own. I needed out, I'm fucking leaving, fucking
leaving tomorrow.

I really hoped I didn't have to wait until Christmas to see Mitten. I loved Mitten more than I've ever loved anyone, but God dammit I hated her guts.

The overhead drip escalates to pouring and it is very evident that we now have a situation.

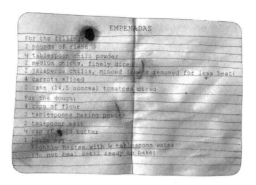

EMPENADAS

For the filling:
2 pounds of flesh
4 tablespoon chili powder
2 medium onions, finely diced
2 jalapenos chilis, minced (seeds removed for less heat)
4 carrots sliced
2 cans (14.5 ounces) tomatoes diced
For the dough:
4 cups of flour
2 tablespoons baking powder
2 teaspoon salt
4 cup of cold butter
1 large egg
lightly beaten with 4 tablespoon water
(do not heat until ready to bake)

8.

I Love the Bronx

It was to be another shameful night spent suffering alone. There wasn't an attractive female in the world that desired to sleep by my side. Not one sexy girl that appreciated or understood my exquisiteness. All the dazzling women were preoccupied spreading themselves open to inferior slobs.

The thought of Tammy doing the deed with a repugnant jock made me feel sick to my stomach. Her beauty was God like, but she didn't care about me or my desires.

Ever since finding Father's pornographic magazines I've become obsessed with sex. During middle school I spent most nights lying on the other side of my sister's door listening while she'd masturbate. The smell of the sexual extract from the vagina was stimulating to me.

I'd been stalking Tammy for weeks at the *House of Gains* where she worked. I'd originally been spending time at the store watching her co-worker Susie Jones. After claiming Susie, I turned my attention to Tammy.

Tammy had a much more athletic physique than Susie, with longer tanned legs. I learned that she lived in Bed Stuy after following her home one night. A very dangerous neighborhood in Brooklyn that a girl like Tammy should never have been found dead in. After I sold the goods to Bunny, that's exactly where I was headed.

The police were under the impression that I was dead, but there'd been numerous reported sightings sparking conspiracies that I was still among the living. I had become an urban myth and it had got to the point that I couldn't leave the house unless I was in disguise.

"Where the hell is Bunny?" I asked myself.

Bunny Goodstuff was a graceless grotesque goblin. I ran into her at a homeless shelter a few years earlier and she became a useful tool to move drugs. She came by my house every morning where I'd sell her five hundred dollars' worth of heroin. I was buying the weekly supply in bulk for twelve hundred, so I was making over two thousand dollars a week in profit. Cash. Still, not one sexy girl in New York City would spend a night with me, not one of them could recognize my elegance or sophistication.

I sat next to the front door closing my eyes and holding my flaccid penis waiting for Bunny. I thought about Susie's final moments and my penis started to erect. Susie Jones was twenty-two years old with the perfect amount of stomach fat when I took her. On the evening I had claimed her, I wore a wig with long beautiful cascading blonde hair and a fifteen-hundred-dollar pair of coruscating Dolce & Gabbana sunglasses. I was willing to give her one more chance to accept me. One more opportunity or pay the ultimate price for rejecting me. I went by the store she worked at in my black and white checkered Prada pants and the tight pink silk shirt was Armani. I can't remember which shoes I wore, but I'm certain they were worth more than she earned in a month. Yet even still, she made no sexual advances towards me.

I tried to engage in conversation, but she focused her attention on another male similar to me in age. It was clear they were flirting and to my utmost disgust she touched his perverted face. When she kissed him on the cheek, I couldn't take it. I watched him put his hand up her shorts grabbing her buttocks and I couldn't accept it. It was torture for me to watch but like a brutal car accident, I couldn't look away. I couldn't comprehend why she would allow this slob to touch her. My blonde wig was worth more than his car and yet she was repulsed by me.

Then I read her lips and was flabbergasted when she muttered, "I want to fuck you."

I couldn't handle it.

The only purchase I made at the store was a gym bag for fifty-two dollars and forty-nine cents that I'd later use to store their body parts. I bought a saw and a crowbar at the hardware store next door and waited outside for her shift to end.

That was the first time I saw Tammy, her co-worker. Like me, Susie's boyfriend was also waiting outside

which devastated me. I watched from across the street as
she leaped into his arms. His arms appeared much bigger
and stronger than mine. She was still wearing the sports
bra and tight short shorts. I was disgusted when the two
of them lit up cigarettes. A terrible habit she had no
doubt picked up from hanging around lower companions
like the one she allowed to touch her buttocks. I
followed them as they walked through Astoria park and
over the Triboro Bridge to Randall's Island. I stayed
twenty steps behind and remained undetected.

They laid down on a patch of grass on Randall's Island
and resumed making out. I sat on a bench and watched
from afar resenting them. The jock started fondling her
breasts, but Susie pulled his hand down and said no. It
seemed for an instant that Susie had come to her senses.
They got back up and walked hand in hand towards the
Hell's Gate Bridge, the most secluded part of the island.

Once the three of us were under the bridge we had
complete privacy. I watched with despair as the jock
pulled up Susie's bra revealing everything. Her nipples
that I had so longed to discover alone were both pierced
with hoop rings. After sucking her tits, he pulled off her
tight shorts, struggling to get them over her voluptuous
body until she was naked. He took his shirt off revealing
his tanned and muscular body and she kissed it. She
unbuckled his jeans dropping his pants and boxers to the
floor. By now his penis, which appeared to be much
more prominent than mine was erect and she put it in her
mouth. He started penetrating her right in front of me. I
got closer to see if she was enjoying herself and it
appeared as though she was. Her moans were getting
louder and her blush face blusher. I could hear and smell
the sex liquids inside her vagina reminding me of when
my sister would masturbate. I picked up my crowbar.

"Fuck me harder." She said not knowing how close I
was to her, how close I was to them.

He turned her around like an animal and spanked her
buttocks yelling random questions like, "Do you like
that you dirty bitch?" She broke my heart when she
responded that she did. I waved the crowbar in the air
until Susie noticed the shadow. When she turned around,
using the crowbar I whacked her ex-boyfriend across the
back of his head. He fell on top of her naked body
trapping her. I started laughing and took my sunglasses
off. She started screaming.

"Help! Help! Somebody help!"

I took the jocks belt off his jeans and tied it around her
neck like a dog, so tight that she stopped screaming. Her
dead ex-boyfriend was covering the parts of her I wanted
to infiltrate, so I had to pull him off. I pulled the belt
tight so she couldn't escape and got on top of her.
Finally, we were together.

"Why are you doing this?!" She said gasping with her
dying eyes.
"Because if I'd asked for permission you would have
said no. You would still have given yourself to him." I
said pointing to her dead ex.

She got quieter and I continued masturbating on her
chest. I could tell she was disappointed with the size of
my penis. When she lost consciousness, I plunged it
inside her already moist vagina and we had sex. I'm not
sure if she died or if I ejaculated first, simultaneously
perhaps. It was close and magical.

After she passed away, using the new saw, I claimed her head before the insects could feed. I also took the jocks head so I could burn it. After I placed the head in my new gym bag, I pulled off Susie's nipple piercing and wore it on my pinky as a souvenir. When I began collecting the meat the sound of children laughing echoed from afar. These sounds of enjoyment reminded me of childhood and happier times before Father left us. The echoes began to ring closer and I was forced to drag the two bodies into the bushes without collecting the organs or meat. I put Susie's bra on her chest to cover her tits incase the children found her. I washed my bloodied hands and peepee in the river before leaving with the heads.

I'd been masturbating for several minutes, unable to ejaculate, and there was still no sign of Bunny Goodstuff. She was twenty minutes late and didn't bother to call. In a fit of rage, I ran to the freezer and took Susie's head out. We went upstairs to my bedroom and I used it to masturbate. I had my peepee in one hand and ran my fingers through her hair with the other. Still no semen. I had five other human heads in the freezer but if Susie couldn't force sperm then I knew the others wouldn't either.

I liked to freeze the heads to keep the flesh intact. Empty skulls never appealed to me. I prefer a detailed face that could still express emotion and more importantly, remorse. I wanted to see it in a girl's face that she regretted not wanting me.

I gave up my eagerness to orgasm and I couldn't continue to wait on Bunny Goodstuff's arrival. It was time to stop kidding around, it was time to get Tammy. It was time to go get what was rightfully mine.

Normally I would put on one of my expensive shirts and sunglass and look wondrous. However, I wanted to blend in so I dressed up as a filthy rotten hipster. I put on a ripped pair of skinny jeans that once belonged to a girl I killed and an *I Love the Bronx* t-shirt. I stuck a fake red beard to my face and drew pig tattoos on my neck and arms. I was ready to go to Brooklyn.

It took me close to an hour to get to Tammy's apartment. She lived above a pretentious artist infested coffee shop with an outdoor patio. I ordered a green tea that tasted like dirt and sat outside waiting for her. Tammy soon walked outside reminding me why I had become so devoted.

She was wearing blue jean shorts, short enough to hide the little cellulite she had developed on her hamstrings and a matching unbuttoned blue button-down shirt over her sports bra. On her way into the coffee shop she high fived some bearded loser. Watching her be so cordial with the guy made me jealous, even though I could tell from his demeanor that he was homosexual. I wanted to stab him for touching her. When she returned with her coffee, she began to converse with him.

"That's a big coffee." The observant gay man said. "What did you get up to last night?"

Then she incinerated me.

"This guy I've been seeing came by, I didn't get much sleep." She said putting her sunglasses on to hide the sin from her eyes.

Her gay friend laughed, which encouraged that type of behavior. How dare she lure me all the way to Brooklyn only to spit in my eye. How dare she give herself to another man while I slept alone staring at her picture. Staring at pictures of her while she gallivanted around different nightclubs, sometimes wearing only lingerie. I decided right then and there that this was the day I'd claim her. She told her gay friend that she was taking the subway to the city, so I went ahead to the station so she didn't detect my pursuit.

On the subway platform was a picture of Susie Jones and some other people I had claimed with the headline *MISSING*. They were missing alright. I wanted to draw a penis in her mouth and write fraud on her forehead, but lacked the convenience of a pen. The sight of Susie's expression aroused me and subtly I began to masturbate while waiting for the J train. I still couldn't orgasm and it was becoming a real problem. Tammy finally came up the steps. I imagined she had gone into further detail about the man she spent the night with and I was enraged. When she finally arrived, I waited for the train engrossed in thoughts of what I was going to do to her.

Had he cum inside of her? I bet he had.
Had he spanked her buttocks? I was certain he would.
Had he sucked her tits and licked cream off her naked body? I couldn't take it.

After we got on the train some disgusting loser holding a beer sat next to her. He started hitting on her and she took off her headphones. As she spoke to him, I could see it in her eyes that she was nothing more than another whore. She smiled as she talked to him. Already, I could tell she was willing to open her legs and give her vagina to him. Even in my hipster costume I looked better than he did. I was a magnificent specimen who spoke eloquently and she was settling for him. I wanted to take my knife out and stab the two of them.

"I'm majestic." I said loud enough for them to hear me.
"What?" The disgusting loser said.
"Why don't you leave her alone?" I said. "You're being obnoxious."
"He's okay." Tammy said.

I tried to slap him, but he punched me twice and I was taking such a beating that Tammy came to my defense telling him to get off. He listened to her and departed the train leaving me with a bloody nose and swollen eye.

"Are you okay?" Tammy asked and I couldn't wait to see what the inside of her head looked like.
"Thank you." I said. "I have a sister so I'm annoyed when I see guys creeping."

I hated my sisters' guts. It was evident from the script she was holding that Tammy was an actress and I knew that nothing got an actress's attention like potential work.

"How bad is my nose?" I asked.
"It's not that bad."
"I'm supposed to be auditioning people this evening, now look at me."
"Auditioning for what?"

And like that, Tammy was mine.

I told her how exciting it was to be directing and producing a new feature film titled, *Waiting for Bunny*. She was intrigued and informed me that she too was an actress. I acted surprised and told her that she had a great look. I could smell semen coming off of her breath and I resented her for it.

"I'm excited to get started." I told her. "Ryan Gosling is a talented guy and I think we will work well together."

She became enticed.

"What time are the auditions?"
 "Six pm." I said knowing that she worked at four.
"Shoot." She said stomping her foot on the floor of the train.
"This might be coming a little out of left field but, would you like to audition?"
"I have to work at four." She exclaimed.
"That's a shame, I think you and Ryan would have had great chemistry together."
"Is there another time I could audition?"

I told her if we moved quickly, she could audition at my apartment and still make it to work on time. She agreed and I started to wonder what the fat on her back was going to taste like.

On the train ride to the Bronx, we became better acquainted. She spoke about her extreme superstition regarding the number thirteen and how she associated her triskaidekaphobia with her mother dying on her thirteenth birthday, on Friday the 13th. Getting to know a girl on a personal level always brought more fulfillment to the claiming. That's my one regret with Susie, I should have got to know her before I took her.

Tammy was from Arizona and had moved to New York a year prior to pursue her acting career. I learned which family members she was closest with and figured out who I could hurt the most. My plan was to not only send pictures of me claiming her to her father's house, but I would send him body parts too, maybe her tongue.

We arrived at my apartment at 1:30 pm. My biggest fear was that Bunny would be there and fuck the whole thing up, but luckily there was still no sign of her. I double locked the door after we entered and Tammy never questioned why. She paid homage to my home and complemented how clean the living room was.

"Looks like a woman's touch." She said unaware of my lonesomeness.

"You're right." I said. "My wife is very organized."

Tammy and I sat on the couch and discussed the film.

"So, who wrote the script?" She asked.

"I did." I said. "I always write the script."

"Wow, what a talented guy." She said and patted me on the back.

Her erotic touch stimulated me.

Before I went upstairs, to get the "scripts", I told her that she needed to prove to Ryan Gosling and myself that she could be comfortable in the most uncomfortable and vulnerable situations.

"What do you have in mind?"

"In the first scene Ryan and yourself are naked in his jacuzzi." I said. "I want you to read the scene with me, naked."

"I barely know you, I'm not taking my clothes off."

"I thought you were serious about this?"

She took off her jean shorts revealing pink see through panties. Then she kicked off her socks and shoes. All she had left was the sports bra and panties.

"All of them." I demanded.
"These too?" she asked.
"Those too."

She took off her bra and panties and sat on the couch crossing her legs.

"You don't seem very comfortable."

She uncrossed her legs and sat back relaxing her shoulders. She dropped her hands down to her knees and I was able to examine her.

"Is that better?" She asked.
"Yes, it is." I said, licking my lips. "I'll be right back."

I ran upstairs to get my hatchet leaving her on the couch. I quickly changed out of my hipster outfit knowing it could get messy. Before re-entering the living room, I hid the weapon behind the door.

"That was weird I couldn't find the scripts."

Tammy had put most of her clothes back on, to my disgust, and told me she didn't want to read the script anymore.

"Was it something I said?" I asked.
"I don't understand why you need me to be naked on the first reading." She said closing the fly on her jean shorts.

I pictured the man she was speaking about in the coffee shop taking her shorts off her and slapping her buttocks the night before. This vision sent me into a rage.

"Because I want to see if you can be comfortable in uncomfortable fucking situations you dirty fucking whore!"

I punched her as hard as I could in the stomach knocking her to the ground and placed my foot on her back. I pressed her down and pulled out my penis. Standing on top of her, I urinated all over her back. I was so angry at this point that I decided I didn't even want to keep the head or the meat. Instead, I wanted to burn her alive in the middle of my living room. I stomped on the back of her head three or four times and was under the impression that she was unconscious. I left her lying in a pool of blood and broken teeth and grabbed a jug of gasoline from the kitchen.

I poured it all over the couch and grabbed a lighter from above the fireplace. I grabbed Tammy by the hair and she spat blood in my face. I threw her on the couch and she bounced back up kicking me in the testicles. While she was trying to unlock the double locked front door, I pulled my gun out from under the coffee table. I put the gun up against the back of her head and told her to get on her knees. When she was on her knees I told her to bend over and kiss my feet. After she kissed my feet, I told her to sit on the couch and she did.

I struggle with rage sometimes but it doesn't last that long. It's usually a short episode. I calmed down and decided that I would take it easy on her and give her an option.

"Listen Tammy, you're going to die right now, but I'm going to let you decide how you go."

"No please." She said, crying hysterically.

"Shut the fuck up!" I yelled. "Either I light this lighter right now and watch you burn to death or I shoot you instead. Your choice."

After a few breaths of crying she pointed to the gun and hung her head. Without hesitation I put the gun against her heart and pulled the trigger.

CLICK!

I forgot to load the gun. Not realizing I had a hatchet behind the door, Tammy jumped up and ran towards the staircase. I followed her and halfway upstairs chopped her right foot off clean. She fell over and started screaming much louder than before.

I dragged her by the hair the rest of the way upstairs into my bedroom and threw her on top of my bed. I loaded the gun in front of her, this time forcing her to take her clothes off. She fainted and I had to take off her pink see through panties myself. I tied her one good foot to the headboard and we spent the next ten minutes having wild sex. After ejaculating I took a knife and cut meat from her right buttock and some from her stomach. I took the flesh downstairs to the kitchen and put it in the oven setting it at 375°.

While it was cooking, I got a bucket and went back upstairs to get blood for my gravy. I found her awake again trying to escape through the window. I took her by her hair and threw her back over the bed.

"You had to put up a fight, didn't you?! Why couldn't you just accept it?!" I screamed.
"Why are you doing this?" She said, falling to the ground.
"Because you chose him and not me."
"Who?"
"Everyone else, but never me, all the other fucking guys but not me!"

While holding her ear tight I whispered in excruciating detail what I was about to do to her.

"I'm going to bend you over right now and slice your throat open. Then, after getting the blood I'll take your head off and put it in the freezer with the six others from before. After that, I'll slice all the meat from your bones and cut your organs out, then I'll have some fun. I'll mail your heart to your dad in Arizona and a kidney each to your aunt and uncle in Portland. Then, I'll personally drive down to Texas and leave your lungs on your mother's grave."

I started laughing.

"When I'm done, I'll put you in a batch of empanadas and feed you to the homeless at the shelter down the block. A bunch of filthy disgusting homeless people eating you with a fork and knife. They'll use a napkin to wipe a piece of your forearm from their chin. How does that sound Tammy?"

I took her silence as ambivalence.

I grabbed her by the hair and slit her throat open like a pig at the slaughter. I stuck her head in the bucket to make sure all the blood was saved. Human blood can make for a really fancy sauce. After she bled out, I picked up the hatchet and took the head in one clean swipe. A lot of blood splattered on the walls and the head fell to the floor rolling under the bed destroying my carpet. I picked up the head and laid back on my bed to examine it. I held it up like a trophy and kissed her on the lips, finally Tammy was mine. The doorbell rang and our moment was spoiled. Bunny fucking Goodstuff.

I took the head and the bucket of blood with me and headed downstairs. When I got to the living room Bunny rang the doorbell again.

"Hold on!" I yelled.

As I placed Tammy's head in the freezer, she rang it again.

"Hold on!"

I checked on the meat and was pleased to see it was cooking nicely. I poured blood and milk into a pot and simmered it for the fancy sauce. She rang the bell for the third time and I thought about smashing her head in. I opened the door and Bunny looked up at me wearing nothing but a blue pillowcase.

"You fucking hobbit."
"I was here earlier. You weren't home."
"What time?" I asked.
"Around nine."

I slapped her in the face with my spatula.

"What time?"
"It could have been closer to ten." She said.

I slapped her again, this time using my fist. She finally conceded that she was over five hours late. I told her to get inside and kicked her in the back as she walked by me.

"How much do you have and what do you need?"
"I have nothing and I need the regular amount."
"What the fuck do you mean you've got nothing?
"They robbed me."
"Who did?"
"Mitten."
"Who the hell is Mitten?"

Bunny described Mitten as some low life waster she'd hired to sell drugs to school children. The night before Mitten drugged Bunny and stole all our inventory. I handed Bunny my iPad and demanded she show me Mitten. She pulled up a picture from her Instagram and gave me back my iPad. I was bedazzled by her goddess beauty. Her eyes were green like the grass in the parks where I used to play as a child, before Father walked out on Mother and me. Her low-cut black top showed off the perfect amount of cleavage for me to fantasize. Then I clicked on the next photograph and was horrified to see her with another man.

"Who's this?" I asked.
"Some other guy." Bunny said, putting her feet up on my couch without examining the picture.

I wanted to crack a match and light the couch on fire with her on it.

First Susie Jones rejected me for an inferior man, then Tammy was up all-night having sex with a rodent she barely even knew and now, Mitten was taking pictures with men like I didn't even exist. I couldn't take it.

"I think she's a lesbian anyway." Bunny said. "She's always going on about some chick called Cindy or something."

Not only was Mitten uninterested, but she was so repulsed by me that she would turn to other females for pleasure.

Instead of lighting Bunny ablaze I killed her with kindness. I needed her alive if I was going to claim Mitten. I offered her some of my empanadas. She said she wasn't hungry but I insisted.

While I was cooking, Bunny went upstairs to wash her hands and desire got the better of me. I started masturbating to the pictures of Mitten on the iPad. I ran to the kitchen and took Tammy's head out of the freezer and started making love to her neck. After a minute or two I saw Bunny's shadow walking behind me, but I couldn't stop. I continued to masturbate for ten more minutes and finally orgasmed. For my pleasure to be sustained, I needed Mitten.

I lit four unscented candles and placed them on the kitchen table using Tammy's head wrapped in a ribbon as the centerpiece. I was nervous Bunny wouldn't like the lunch and was relieved when she expressed her utter fulfillment. She expressed so much interest in the dish that I wrote out the recipe for her, warning her to not undercook the flesh. Right as we were about to discuss business, I remembered that I'd forgotten to get a bottle of wine.

I went downstairs to the cellar and got a bottle of the Cote De Rhone, an impeccable balanced red wine from the Lyon region in the south of France. It tasted like a mouthful of my childhood reminding me of when my mother used to take us swimming in the Gulf of Mexico. She was such a strong-minded woman. The empanadas were cooked perfectly, the meat was moist and even Tammy would have appreciated the flavors, if she'd lived to taste it.

I shared my plan with Bunny.

"I'm going to claim Mitten tonight."

She understood and we arranged to meet at Tompkins Square Park at Midnight. Bunny's job was to lure Mitten there, where I'd claim her. Bunny had lost her cell phone so we concluded that she would lure her to the north east side of the park.

I knew Tammy's body would be starting to rot so I excused myself and asked Bunny to let herself out after I handed her the heroin to sell.

"You owe me a thousand." I warned her, before she left.

I grabbed my crowbar and a sledge hammer from under the sink and got some newspaper from the bathroom. The first step was breaking the rib cage open to get to the organs. I did this by smashing the back of the body with the sledge hammer and then wedged it open with the crowbar. I took out the heart first and wrapped it in two pages of the New York Times. Next came the liver and both kidneys, also wrapping them in paper. The lungs were trickier. One of them got damaged on the way out. I put each in a small cardboard box and spent the next hour looking for their addresses online. I figured I'd freeze the lungs for a few months before following through with the promise to leave them on her mother's grave. After I packaged all the organs, I started to take the meat. The body was lacking in fat but because of her young age I was very pleased with how tender the meat was. I took all the meat from around the buttocks and stomach and put it in the fridge for myself. The rest was going into the batch of the empanadas for the shelter. Once I'd taken all the meat, I put the rest of the skeleton into the bathtub and filled it up with hydrochloric acid. I left her there deteriorating while I cooked up a feast in the kitchen. The entire process took me about four hours.

I photographed multiple pictures of myself opening the body to send to her family members along with the organs. I'd bought a beautiful instant print camera which had now proved useful. My favorite picture was the one of her hand with her rings still on. It felt so real to me. I snapped another classic after breaking her back open with the sledge hammer and another one of her head on the dinner table. While the meat was still in the oven, I cleaned myself up and brought the cardboard boxes with the organs and pictures to the post office and mailed them to their recipients accordingly. Before leaving, I was furious to discover Bunny had deceived me by stealing Tammy's jeans shorts. I was relieved she hadn't taken the underwear though and put them in my pocket for safekeeping.

When I returned from the post office Tammy's meat was ready to become an empanada. I changed into my chef costume and made my way to the shelter.

My "pork" empanadas were always a huge hit and my popularity was transcending at the shelter. A black man

that ran the haven always welcomed me with a
handshake. He smelled so foul that I would have to rush
home and shower just from being in his presence.

"Enjoy lunch?" I said watching him take a bite. A piece
of meat was stuck to his teeth as he said goodbye.

I thought about what could have been, if only Tammy
had given herself to me.

After getting home I reopened my iPad and stalked
Mitten's Facebook and Instagram more extensively.
After thorough research, I realized Mitten had
heterochromia. Her right eye was green and the left
greenish blue. I couldn't even fathom the idea of having
a head in the freezer with two different eye colors. The
stalking included binge masturbation, but this time I was
unable to climax. I couldn't get the image of another pair
of hands touching Mitten's body out of my head. I
couldn't accept it.

An hour of sexual frustration later I started doubting
Bunny's legitimacy. How could I trust her to lure Mitten
to the park after she stole the jean shorts? I couldn't. I
decided the only way to get Mitten's attention was by
claiming her myself. Her Facebook profile had limited
information on where she could be found. She hadn't
posted a single thing on there since a picture of a
Christmas tree in 2014, and I assumed it was because
she was too busy spreading her legs and opening her
vagina to others. I changed back into my hipster outfit
and headed to the Village.

I figured if Mitten knew Bunny Goodstuff then
Tompkins Square Park was a good starting point to
begin the hunt. Manhattan is a cesspit and being there

was screwing up my psychology. When I was halfway up the steps at Union Square train station a large withered rat walked by my shoe holding half a burrito in his mouth. Welcome to Manhattan.

In route to the park, I made a pit stop at the *Best Buy* on 14th Street and masturbated in the women's bathroom. Yet another orgasm prevented by the thought of Mitten's naked body being touched by someone else. Our life could be so easy if she had the decency to give herself to me.

"These breasts belong to you Thomas!" She would take off her top and yell at the top of her lungs.
"Whose tits are those?" I'd say while pointing to them, touching both nipples with my index fingers.
"They're yours." She'd say.

I'd have ejaculated all over them, but no. That isn't how it would ever pan out. Instead, she would ignore me and give herself to someone else. Anyone but me, anyone but Thomas.

While stroking my penis thinking about all this, a young woman entered the stall next to me. I stood on the toilet and watched her urinate. She was too busy on her phone to notice me. Of course, no women ever noticed me so why would she be any exception.

After leaving *Best Buy*, I stopped by *The Bean* for a green tea. The female barista was wearing a red bandana on her head teasing me. I tried to speak with her after ordering, but she looked at me like I was an inferior ghost and instead she chatted to her disgusting coworker. He had tarnished his skin with ink and looked obese. His stomach was so large that his shirt couldn't cover his belly button and his belt was unable to keep his pants up, forcing us all to have to witness the crack of his buttocks. I couldn't understand it. Was I that ghastly that we couldn't even participate in a conversation?

"I'll be back tomorrow." I said.
"Good." She said, if only she knew what I was going to do.

I walked from *The Bean* to Tompkins Square Park, drinking my green tea and sniffing Tammy's pink see through underwear. The panties reminded me of when I was a child sitting outside my sister's door, listening to her.

A young couple around my age were sitting on a bench making out. I sat next to them and observed. They both kept their eyes shut as they kissed and I was able to take a good close look. She put her hand on his leg and I could see from the motion in his trousers that he was aroused. I could also tell from the movement that he too had a bigger and stronger penis than mine. My guess was that they would have sex later that night. They left soon after and if I hadn't been looking for Mitten, I'd have followed them home.

The sun had set and many sexy girls were out in their fancy short dresses showing off serious cleavage that I couldn't handle. For years I'd wished that there was a law that woman had to cover all their skin. It was unfair that they could walk around half naked and alpha males like me were supposed to somehow control themselves. Any woman with a dress showing their knees or a shirt showing shoulders or God forbid breasts should have been classified as free fair game to a man of my stature. I was so frustrated that I had to hide behind a tree to try and relieve myself. As I played with my penis, I saw a boom box that looked like it was twenty years old. I pressed the play button and some black music started blasting. Two females nearby seemed pleased and gave me a wave. I turned it up louder and started to dance. The girls continued to wave and one of them shook her hips. Had I found a solution? Then out of nowhere a black man grabbed me by the shoulders and flung me onto the ground.

"Let me go!" I screamed at the bigger one of the two.

He pushed me in the face and I told him that he was acting like a lunatic

"Get off me!" I begged.

While I was pressed to the ground, I noticed her. Mitten, walking through the park without a care in the world. She looked more beautiful in person than she had in the pictures.

"Get off me!" I yelled, and this time he did. I jumped to my feet and ran after Mitten.

She was dressed in all black and was a fast New York walker.

During the pursuit, I began fantasizing about holding her head, the blood dripping from her detached throat bouncing off her dead body beneath it. The nipples still hard and her vagina so alive as I penetrated her dead body from behind. The meat coming off the bone so tender you could cut it with a spoon.

There are many misconceptions about the taste of human meat. First of all, humans do not taste like chicken, to be perfectly honest we don't even taste that much like pork, but with the right spices and flavoring you can make it quite similar. The closest comparison is veal, in fact it's indistinguishable and if you blind tasted someone there's no way they could tell the difference. The human diet is imperative to the taste of the meat, if they're drinking soda or eating fried food, the taste of the meat will dwindle. I could tell from her state that Mitten took great care of herself and would taste delicious.

I got a call from Bunny Goodstuff.

"She's going to be at the park at midnight."
"I'm already following her." I said. "Distract her and I'll claim her from behind."

I hung up and continued to follow her. I was upset to see Mitten enter an AA meeting. Alcoholics Anonymous was full of disgusting losers and I couldn't accept than Mitten was like them. Considering her sexual indecisiveness, it was hardly any great surprise that she had self-control issues. I waited outside the meeting for its entirety and at one point masturbated to no avail behind a parked car. Despite chewing on Tammy's panties, I couldn't discharge. Tammy was old news I needed to be chewing on Mittens intimate lingerie. The lack of semen produced upset me and caused me to dump Tammy's pink panties in a nearby trash can. By now all the disgusting homeless peasants at the shelter would be digesting her and her organs were on a plane to Arizona. It was a sweet victory indeed.

I started to go over the logistics and thought about what white wine I would drink on the side. From her appearance, I figured perhaps I'd try a new Pinot Grigio, a zesty white wine from the Lombardy region in Northern Italy.

People started to disperse from the meeting and by then I was impatient and frustrated. Fleets of people were saying their goodbyes, but there was no sign of Mitten.

"Are there more people inside?" I asked an old hag. "No." She said, "We are the last to leave."

I couldn't accept it.

When I turned around, I couldn't believe my fucking eyes. The motherfucker from the train who assaulted me was standing right in front of me. He was incoherent and could only stand with the aid of some monster in a skinny scarf. I punched him in the face returning the favor from the J train and ran down the block.

"What the fuck was that?!" His tall bald friend yelled as I ran.

I looked up and down the block, but there was no sign of Mitten anywhere. No trace of her green and greenish blue eyes. Suddenly, I realized there were cops everywhere. First Bunny Goodstuff took Tammy's blue jean shorts without permission and now she had deceived me for the second and final time.

Every damn cop in the East Village was after me. As I ran east, I heard them firing two warning shots towards me. A third quickly followed. When I got to Coopers Square, I hid under a park bench and pretended to be asleep.

Coopers Square was filled with trees and leaves that reminded me of vacationing with my parents when I was a child. I was happy when we were all together, eating hot dogs with mustard and the smell of Fathers cigarettes on his clothes. Life was good before the incident, before Father allowed them to touch me.

I saw a clock in the distance that read midnight. It seemed like I'd lost the cops and it was time for Goodstuff to feel my wrath. I figured she had told them where I lived so going home was no longer on the table. I checked that my gun was loaded and walked to Tompkins Square Park.

The number one rule in New York is that you don't go to the park at night because it's full of creeps. When I got there, it was deserted with the exception of a few homeless losers sleeping. The sounds of the vagrants snoring and the rats squeaking echoed through the stuffy air.

I sat on the bench next to a trash can in the north west side of the park and outlined my next move. As I peeled off my fake beard, Bunny appeared from the abyss, still dressed in the outlandish blue pillowcase.

"Hey Chef."
"Where's Mitten?" I demanded.
"She hasn't shown up."
"Imagine that." I said.
"Maybe she went to the other side of the park?"
"Perhaps she did."

Bunny turned around and started walking to the other side of the park. I pulled out my handgun and shot her in the back. She fell to the ground speechless, trying to reach to the bullet hole with her short hands. I kicked her in the back.

"What the fuck?!" She muttered.

I kicked her around like a football a few more times demanding the truth.

"Was Mitten in on this too?" I asked. "Did you both try and fuck me?"
"What are you…"

I stepped on her mouth so she couldn't talk and burnt her cheek with the top of my gun.

"You set me up you little dwarf bitch!"

I pointed my gun at her tiny head and called her a grotesque gruesome goblin for the last time. Just as I was about to pull the trigger, someone called my name.

"Tommy!"
"It's Thomas." I said as I turned around. "Who the fuck are you?"
 "Put the gun down."

I recognized him immediately, it was the less big of the two men who jumped me, the one who helped pull his bigger friend off of me.

"What, are you a fucking cop?"
"Yeah." He said, flashing his badge.
"Well she's my property so it's none of your business what I'm doing here."
"Define property?" He asked.
"To which a person owns, possessions."

"Drop the weapon Tommy."
"For the last time my name is Thomas."
"Thomas, drop the gun."
"No."

I point my gun right at him and pull the trigger.

9.

Dorothy's Dead

CRACK!

Max shot the bald fucker with the skinny scarf for the third time, this time splattering his head all over the pavement.

"What did I fucking tell you?!" Bigley screamed. "You fucking idiot."
"Show some respect." I said to Bigley.
"Respect?" Bigley said, pointing to Max and adding. "A black fucking cop just shot an unarmed civilian that he shot twice already."
"That scumbag killed Dorothy." I said.
"Innocent until proven guilty." He explained.

While we were arguing Max was on the ground searching his pockets.

"Guilty." Max said handing Billy the tip of the other dead girl's finger.
"Put it in a fucking bag before it rots!" Bigley yelled.

Max would have to go back to the precinct to give a statement. I didn't know whether to say thank you or punch him in the face, so I didn't say anything at all.

"Someone needs to clean up this fucking mess!" Billy yelled pointing to the ground.

Max was forced to go by the precinct to fill out forms and I feared for the worst. What a mess. First I lost Dorothy and now I was on the brink of losing Max.

After starting the car, *Shelter from the Storm* came on, taking me back to the night we waited for the rain to clear. The night I fell in love. Her husband's death didn't diminish the pain and it seemed to only start to kick in that she was gone. I took all the CD's out of the glove compartment and spread them across the passenger seat, where they were the night we met. I closed my eyes and imagined she was sitting beside me. I drove to Tompkins Square Park to retrieve the boombox.

The boombox was exactly where we left it. I sat next to the tree and allowed the tears to run down my face. I called Dorothy's cell phone and listened to her recorded voice. I listened to the most recent voicemail she left me.

"Hey, I'm sorry you had to leave early. I had a wonderful night, I hope I didn't ruin it by asking you to leave. I wish you could have stayed. He has to go to court in the morning so I'll text you as soon as he leaves. Mitten is coming too, hopefully with good news. This isn't going to be like this forever. I think I heard him pull in. I better go, I love you."

As I was about to listen to it for the eighth time, I heard a bunch of commotion coming from nearby. I went to check and just like that, there she was. Bunny Goodstuff. She was sitting on a park bench beside the homeless guy in the *I Love the Bronx* t-shirt. I couldn't tell why at first, but he looked different. After he shouted at Bunny, she stood up and started walking north. I started to follow her but out of nowhere, he shot Bunny in the back. That's when I realized it was him. Tommy "Chef" Fogarty was standing over Bunny Goodstuff with a fucking gun in his hand. My feet were frozen, stuck in the mud with fear. Chef was using the top of his gun to burn Bunny's face screaming something about how she'd deceived him and how someone didn't ever exist. Without thinking, I yelled his name. I was still holding the boombox.

"Tommy!"
"Who the fuck are you?"
"Put the gun down." I said in a calm voice.

He got off Bunny, now holding his gun down by his side.

"What are you a fucking cop? He asked.

I flashed my badge.

"What's with the boombox?"
"Tommy put the gun down."
"My name is Thomas." He said. "Only Father calls me Tommy."

He pointed his gun at me and I watched in what felt like slow motion as he pulled the trigger. I fired a shot back at him falling to the ground. I laid on my back and stared through the street lights at the night's sky. I was back at the bowling alley on our second date.

"What was the best day of your life?" Dorothy asked me.
"My first day at school." I lied, because I feared I'd have sounded like a loser if she heard the truth, it was really two nights ago when we met.
"Why school? I hated school." She said.
"I was an only child so it was a relief to just be around other kids."
"I hated all the kids at my school." She said.
"Yeah, but it beats being alone."

Lying in the gravel I checked my body for bullet holes. So far so good, I thought to myself before checking my legs. No holes. I radioed for backup.

"Shots fired in Tompkins Square Park."

Tommy was lying a few feet away from me dead in the gutter. I was closing his eyes with my fingers when I heard her.

"I know you."

I turned around and saw a young woman staring at me.

"Who are you?"
"I'm Mitten."

It was Dorothy's private detective. I had so many questions but we had so little time.

"I'm looking for my brother." She said.

The sound of sirens started ringing around the park. I handed Mitten my card and told her to email me his information.

"I have a couple of bodies to attend to." I said hinting that she should move along.
"There's only one body." Mitten said. "Unless you're talking about that dead rat."

Bunny Goodstuff was gone. When I turned around Mitten was already on her way out the park. I found something on the ground where Bunny had been lying. It was an envelope ripped open. On one side was a handwritten recipe:

For the filling:
2 pounds of flesh
½ tablespoon chili powder
2 medium onions, finely diced
2 jalapenos chilis, minced (seeds removed for less heat)
4 carrots sliced
2 cans (14.5 ounces) tomatoes diced

For the dough:
4 cups of flour
2 tablespoons baking powder
2 teaspoons salt
½ cup of cold butter
1 large egg, lightly beaten with ½ tablespoon water (do not beat until ready to bake)

And on the other side were cooking instructions and an address:

123 East Gun Hill Road
Bronx, New York 10467

I put it my pocket before anyone showed up. The sirens got louder and Bigley was one of the first on the scene.

"Another fucking body?!" He screamed.
"Look who it is." I said.
"I don't give a fuck who it is."
"It's the Chef."
"Fogarty's dead."
"Now he is."

Bigley examined the body and his tone switched, he pointed at Bunny's puddle of blood.

"What's this?"
"He shot Bunny Goodstuff."
"He shot her?"
"He did."
"Where is she?"
"She got away."

His tone switched again.

"She's a four-foot fucking dwarf." Bigley screamed.
"How the fuck did she get away?"

It didn't matter that I'd brought down the most notorious serial killer since Ted Bundy, Bigley was obsessed with Bunny Goodstuff.

"One thing at a time man." I said. "We'll get her tomorrow."

Once the forensics team showed up, I picked up the boombox and went back to the precinct to see Max. He was sitting in the dining room drinking a can of coke alone. Before he noticed me, I hit play on the boombox.

"I hate that fucking song." Max said.

I put the recipe on the table.

"Look what I found."
"I'm not hungry man."
"Read it."

Max read the recipe and like me was confused with the description of the protein. *2 pounds of flesh.*

"Who calls beef flesh?"

I filled him in on what had occurred at the park and on who he had been beating up at Tompkins Square Park. Max was facing suspension for killing the bald fucker in the purple scarf. However, if we were able to find Tammy or one of the other missing people at this address, that would stand well in court. We agreed to withhold the information from Bigley and drove up to the Bronx ourselves.

"How does Tommy know Bunny though?" Max asked during the commute.
"That's what we are going to find out Max."

We pulled up on East Gun Hill Road outside the house in darkness. The only exception was a light on upstairs, in what appeared to be the bathroom. With a gun in one hand and a flashlight in the other we each made our way to the house.

Max kicked the door in and turned the lights on. The first thing we noticed was a blue pillowcase covered in blood on the couch. On the staircase, we found a human foot that was being devoured by ants. The nails were painted black suggesting it was possibly once a woman.

We both walked upstairs and entered the bedroom with our guns still drawn. The sheets on the bed, the floor and the walls were soaked in blood. The hatchet and knife on the floor were also painted in blood, indicating that a serious, sinister action had occurred there.

"What the fuck happened here?" Max asked.

After entering the bathroom, we found the bathtub full of acid with something still dissolving inside it. We went back downstairs to the kitchen and found more blood on the counter.

"We have to call Bigley." I said to Max and he agreed.

While I was on the phone to the Sarge, Max continued the investigation. I'd just given Bigley the address when I heard him screaming from another room. I hung up the phone and Max ran back out coming towards me.

"Don't fucking go in there." Max said pointing to the laundry room.

I wish I had listened.

There were six human heads in his freezer, including Susie Jones and Quincy Quinn. When I returned to the living room Max was sitting on the couch. I joined him and we waited for backup.

"Why does this couch smell so bad?" I asked.
"I don't want to know." Max said.

We sat in silence for a minute and tried to take in the day that we just had. Max pulled out a cigarette and put it in his mouth and I wasn't going to try and stop him. He searched his pockets looking for a lighter. I picked up a book of matches from the coffee table and asked him to give me a smoke.

"Since when did you start smoking?" He asked.
"You only live once."

I took the cigarette from Max's mouth and put it in my own. As I was about to crack the match my phone vibrated with an email from Mitten. I opened it. Max took the book of matches from my hand and lit another cigarette. Mitten's email was titled *Sweet Philip* and I scrolled down. A photograph was attached. I opened it and was surprised to see a picture of Phil, the junkie from Thompkins Square Park.

Max inhales.

The End.

About the Author

Seanie Sugrue is originally from Tralee, County Kerry in Ireland. In March 2005 he moved to New York City, where he spent the following thirteen years. In 2014 while producing the feature film Catch 22: based on the unwritten story by seanie sugrue, he wrote his first play Black Me Out!. In the summer of 2016 after directing his fourth play Love is Dead!, which later became a feature film, he began writing his debut novel, Cardboard Coffins. Shortly after writing and directing the feature film Misty Button, Sugrue turned his attention back to the book and finished it in the fall of 2018. Seanie currently resides in Los Angeles, California.

Made in the USA
Columbia, SC
15 August 2020

16473120R00120